REST

A Death au Jour Mystery #2

Hillary Avis

©2018 Hillary Avis www.hillaryavis.com
ISBN 9781099380921

This book is a work of fiction. Any resemblance to real people, places, events, or organizations is purely coincidental, and all are the creation of the author.

Cover by Mariah Sinclair www.mariahsinclair.com
Editing by Anna Hight
For permissions contact: books@hilyardpress.com

Chapter 1

Bethany Bradstreet leaned over the stock pot and inhaled the intoxicating scent of her latest creation. It was almost ready—she just had to whisk in the eggs and lemon juice. She scooped out a few cups of steaming broth into a mixing bowl.

"Do you have a sec to pour for me?"

"Why don't you use the whisk attachment for the mixer?" Kimmy asked, wiping her hands on her Café Sabine apron.

Bethany shrugged. "I don't know—I just like to do things by hand. For some reason it tastes different."

"You're right. I can always tell when chefs use some elbow grease. I'd never get plates in front of diners if I did everything by hand, though." Kimmy poured a slow, steady stream of beaten eggs into the broth while Bethany furiously beat the mixture with a whisk so the eggs wouldn't curdle in the hot soup. "Avgolemono—brave choice. How are you going to make sure it doesn't turn into scrambled eggs while you serve it?"

Bethany laughed. "Very careful babysitting. That's the upside of only making one soup per day! It gets all the love."

"I want some love!" Charley poked her head through the swinging doors of the kitchen. Kimmy rolled her eyes and gave her girlfriend a peck on the lips. Charley shook her head. "No—I meant I want some of Bethany's soup."

Kimmy's mouth dropped open in mock dismay. "Should I be jealous that you like Bethany's cooking better than mine?"

Charley blinked innocently. "Why would you think that?"

"I don't know, because you come by the café every morning now that Bethany makes her soup here, when you never did before?"

Charley kissed Kimmy again. "You know I like your home cooking. All the French stuff here is too fancy for me, though. Give me a bowl of comfort food any day."

Bethany ladled out two servings of the avgolemono and added a pinch of chopped herbs to the top of each. "What would I do without my two professional tasters?" she asked, hoping to stop their argument before it started. She handed them each a spoon.

"Fine." Kimmy rolled her eyes and dipped her spoon into the bowl. "Oh, wow, Bethany! This is fantastic. Just the right amount of lemon—and those herbs! Marjoram?"

Bethany nodded.

"Mmm," Charley said. "What did you say this was? Avoca-do-mole?"

"Avgolemono," Bethany said. "It's Greek."

"Well, it's all-good-emono if you ask me." Charley glanced at her watch. "Can I take it to go? I've gotta get to work."

"Shoot, is it that time already?" Bethany slammed a lid on the stock pot and heaved it onto a dolly. "Come by the kiosk later—law enforcement eats free."

"Better not tell my buddies that, or you won't have any left for paying customers." Charley grinned at Bethany and then tugged the ends of Kimmy's braids. "I'll see you later, hon."

"Hm." Kimmy crossed her arms. "Will you?"

Charley batted her eyelashes. "I don't know—are you going to make those yummy little cookies dipped in chocolate?"

Kimmy motioned to the rows of madeleines cooling on a rack behind her. "Every day."

"Then you will definitely see me later. Want help loading, Bethany?"

Bethany nodded. "I could use a hand. Thanks for letting me cook here, Kimmy."

Kimmy patted her on the back. "Don't let Charley eat it all on the way out."

Together, Charley and Bethany wheeled the dolly out the back door of Café Sabine and loaded the stock pot onto the cargo trailer hitched to Bethany's yellow bike.

Charley waved as she mounted her own bike and headed off to the police station. Bethany locked the empty dolly to the bike rack and gingerly pedaled across the street to the train station, careful not to jar the trailer as she navigated the curb and a manhole cover. She dismounted and pushed her bike through a vaulted entrance that seemed a little too grand for such a small depot.

Newbridge Station was as old as the town, but it was tiny—only a single platform in each direction, and the Zam-Rail trains only ran on weekdays, mostly to service commuters headed to New Haven. The compact concourse housed a small bakery, the ticket office, and a circle of antique benches for passengers to wait on, and not much else. The Souperb Soups kiosk, Bethany's pride and joy, was squeezed against the wall across from the bakery with another kiosk. Nothing in the station was glamorous except the beautiful arched entryway and vaulted ceiling. Still, it was a lovely, historic building with enough foot traffic that Bethany's business was brisk.

She wheeled the bike to the back of her kiosk and unloaded the avgolemono onto the warmer, careful not to scuff the worn marble floor. She lit the burner and turned it down as low as it would go so the eggs wouldn't curdle in the broth. "OK, little soup—be good while I lock up old Daisy, here."

When she got back, a small line was already forming by her booth, but before she could get behind the counter and start serving, Olive flew out of the Honor Roll Bakery toward her, turquoise earrings jangling and her hands fluttering wildly.

"Oh, honey!" she said, her large brown eyes full of concern. "Don't look. Just ignore her."

"What is it? Is something wrong?"

Olive put her hand to her mouth, a deep crease forming between her eyebrows. "Oh, I can't even say it—I don't want it to be true. It's just too much. *She's* just too much."

Bethany groaned. "Say no more." She knew exactly who Olive was talking about—only one person in Newbridge was too much for Olive, and that was Marigold Wonder. She rented the kiosk next to Bethany's and made weird smoothies that were supposed to be healthy out of things like mushrooms and algae. During Marigold's grand opening last fall, she'd handed out pamphlets of anti-gluten propaganda that Olive did *not* appreciate, to put it mildly. "What's she making now, dirt smoothies?"

"Maybe you can hang up a curtain so you don't have to see it," Olive said.

Bethany glanced over at Marigold's kiosk and almost fell on the floor. The booth was shrouded in canvas and had a big banner that said "CLOSED—Grand Re-Opening Tomorrow."

Marigold was teetering on a ladder as she installed a new sign: Souperior Soups.

"You have *got* to be kidding me!"

Olive shook her head. "I know. I *know*."

Bethany marched over to the base of the ladder. "What the heck, Marigold?!"

"Isn't it amazing?" Marigold picked her way down the ladder, carefully placing her spiked heels on each rung, and gazed up at the sign admiringly. "Newbridge isn't very health conscious, so the smoothies weren't really working out here. I looked at your lines"—she motioned to the people standing at Bethany's kiosk—"and I knew a good idea when I saw one!"

"Maybe if you made your smoothies out of something other than sticks and leaves—" Bethany sputtered.

"Too late now, I already changed the sign. Anyway, making soup is going to be fun! We can be soup buddies. Do you have a mirror? I probably look awful after sweating over all the renovations." Marigold fluffed her bleach-blonde curls, her fingers sparkling with rings. "Oh—look who I'm asking. Of course you don't."

Bethany's mouth opened and closed a few times. She didn't know how to respond to that. Thank goodness for Olive, who bustled over and herded Bethany back to her kiosk before she said something she'd regret.

"Hush now, just serve your soup like you always do. After lunch, go to the stationmaster's office and file a complaint. You know Ben didn't approve this!"

Wordlessly, Bethany went through the motions of setting up her kiosk as fast as she could. She wrote "Avgolemono" on the chalkboard, tied on her Souperb Soups apron, and set out her "Soup's On" sign.

"It's about time," the first customer in line said.

Bethany nodded apologetically. "Sorry about the wait. I think this one will be worth it, though." The avgolemono was still looking creamy and perfect, the fresh scent of lemon and herbs lingering on its surface, the comforting chew of orzo floating underneath. Just right for a bright winter day.

"Can I get bread with this?" a tall, thin man she didn't recognize asked. *First-timer.*

Bethany pointed to the bakery just a few feet away. "The Honor Roll has the best bread. Ask Olive for something to go with the soup—she's great at pairings."

"Thanks!" The man headed for the bakery, his steaming container of soup in hand. *Wouldn't be surprised to see him back tomorrow,* Bethany thought, as she served soup to the long line of loyal customers. One of them even proclaimed the avgolemono her "best soup yet," and he'd tried them all.

"Lots of happy diners today," Charley said, leaning on the counter. "Did I miss my chance for lunch?"

"Nope, still got a bowl or two. The bottom of the pot is always the best, anyway." Bethany ladled a generous portion into a to-go container and paused with her hand on a second container. "Do you want to take some for Coop?" Andrew Cooper was Charley's partner and never passed up a free meal.

Charley shook her head. "He's off for the week. Went to Vegas to get married, the lazy bum!"

"It's a good thing—I'm not sure I had enough left for both of you!" Bethany grinned and handed the container of soup to Charley with a spoon. "Here you go—on the house."

"Yikes, sold out and it's not even noon. You better start making two pots of soup."

Bethany grinned. "I don't know. A one-hour workday isn't so bad."

Charley rolled her eyes. "You work a lot more than one hour. Think about all the time you spend in the kitchen!"

"Doesn't feel like work, I guess."

"Um, excuse me?" the customer in line behind Charley piped up. "Are you really out of soup?"

"See you later," Bethany said to Charley, and then raised her voice so the person behind Charley could hear. "No, ma'am, still have enough for you." Charley moved aside, affording Bethany a view of the customer, and Bethany froze.

"Oh, thank goodness," Marigold said. She plunked her bedazzled purse on the counter and pulled out an overstuffed wallet. "I just had to try it—it smells so good. How much do you charge?"

Bethany put the lid back on the stock pot with a *clang*. "Why do you want to know? So you can charge less for yours?"

Marigold waved her hand. "Oh, no. I'll charge exactly the same. I wanted to know so I can pay you."

"Oh," Bethany said in a small voice. Of course, Marigold just wanted lunch—there was no reason to be so suspicious all the time. "No charge, Marigold. I hope you enjoy it."

"Well, aren't you a peach?" Marigold took the bowl of soup and slurped it noisily. Bethany tucked away her "Soup's On" sign and erased the chalkboard now that the avgolemono was gone. Marigold licked her spoon and pointed it at Bethany. "This is some excellent soup. You know what would be a blast?"

Knowing Marigold, she probably meant putting glitter on something that should not be glittery. "No, what?"

"We should soup-swap every day! We can trade our soups-of-the-day so we can taste each other's recipes."

Bethany needed to eat more soup like she needed a hole in the head, but figured it wasn't worth discussing the finer points of her diet with Marigold. "Sure. Uh, fine—as long as your soup doesn't have algae in it."

"You're such a silly-goose!" Marigold poked her spoon at Bethany again. "Silly-willy-billy-goose! Oh, we are going to have so much fun. Toodles, soup sister!"

"Kill me now," Bethany muttered under her breath as soon as Marigold left. She carried the stock pot back across the street to Café Sabine, where Kimmy was in the middle of the lunch rush. She peeked into the dining room and saw the café packed with people having business meetings and lunch dates.

Kimmy's definitely too busy to chat. Bethany would have to tell her about Marigold's shenanigans that night when Kimmy got home from work.

Bethany and Kimmy had been roommates since graduation from culinary school and often had a drink—whether herbal tea or something stiffer—at the end of the day, a ritual they started back when they were both first-year chefs learning to sharpen their knives. Even now that Kimmy was dating Charley, they still made time for it if they could.

"I'm all sold out across the street. Can I pitch in and help?" she asked. Kimmy seemed to be stirring four pans at once.

Kimmy shook her head, never taking her eyes from the stove. "Nope. If Monsieur Adrien wants me to get food out faster, he needs to hire a *chef de partie*."

"OK, suit yourself. See you at home after dinner service."

Bethany eyed her yellow bike locked up in the alley next to Café Sabine's recycling bin. It was the perfect day to take Daisy out—sunny and bright, despite the cold. Unfortunately, Bethany had some business to take care of before she could ride on her favorite route along the waterfront.

Time to talk to Ben about the kiosk situation. She sighed. She hated to be a complainer, but she also didn't think Marigold was really being a team player. Bethany *could* be serving bread with her soup and Olive *could* be making soup to go with her sandwiches and rolls, but they weren't. If Marigold wanted her kiosk to succeed, she needed to find synergy with Souperb Soups and Honor Roll—not compete directly with them. Really, Bethany was doing her a favor by filing a complaint.

She knocked briskly at the door to the stationmaster's office. Ben Kovac answered, his collar unbuttoned and his eyes so weary they made his face look like a Basset hound's.

"Make it snappy. I have to do the track maintenance before the 1:55 comes in," he grumbled, motioning her into the office where Caboose, Newbridge Station's fluffy orange mouser, lay curled up on his desk.

Bethany scratched the cat's chin and he stretched out, purring, so she could better reach his belly. "Why isn't Trevor doing it?"

"*Trevor*," Ben said derisively, "hasn't finished the sprinkler system repairs, and I can't pull him off that because it's a safety violation. So I'm stuck doing his job *and* mine. What do you want?"

"Marigold changed her kiosk name."

"So?"

Bethany shifted uncomfortably. "To Souperior Soups. She's basically made her kiosk a carbon copy of mine. Can you talk to her about it?"

Ben sighed. "Can't you talk to her first?"

"I did! She seems pretty gung-ho. And I'd rather not file a complaint with ZamRail if I can avoid it..." She hoped that leaning on his distaste for paperwork would motivate him to put the kibosh on Marigold's new venture.

Ben threw up his hands. "Just what I need. It's not enough that this building is crumbling around my ears, now I have a soup mutiny." He picked up a keyring bristling with keys, and Caboose startled at the noise, jumping off the desk onto the office floor. "Listen, the fleabag and I have to do the rounds. But I'll bring it up with Marigold tonight at our weekly poker game. She's usually more open to discussion when she's had a couple of martinis. Maybe I can talk her out of it."

Bethany smiled. "Thanks, Ben. I owe you one."

"Everybody owes me one," Ben muttered as he and the cat followed her out. "Wish some of them would pay up."

• • • •

"MARIGOLD IS A SHADY lady." Kimmy shook her head disbelievingly. "'Souperior Soups'? Superior to whose?"

"Mine, I guess." Bethany heaved a sigh and took a sip of her chamomile tea.

"Not possible. Has she ever made a soup in her life?"

"Who knows. Smoothies are kind of like soup. I mean, I blend some soups. And there are fruit soups, like cold dessert ones. So maybe she's right, and hers will be 'souperior.'" She made air quotes around the word.

Kimmy pulled a patchwork quilt over her lap and snuggled into the shabby green sofa. "You are just making excuses for her now. On Julia Child's grave, I swear I've never had better soups than yours. That Greek one you made this morning blew my *mind*, it was so good. You have nothing to be worried about."

Bethany put her tea down on the coffee table. "What am I going to do if my kiosk closes, Kimmy? No restaurant will hire me in this town, not after what happened last year."

"Nobody remembers that." Kimmy gave her a sympathetic look. "And if they do, they also remember that you didn't do anything wrong."

Bethany shook her head and willed herself not to cry. "That kind of rep sticks with you. No restaurant wants that notoriety."

Kimmy scooted over and put her arm around Bethany's shoulders. "Come on, now. That's your fear talking. You're thinking like ten catastrophes into the future. Some shady lady is not going to put you out of business. She'll try, and you will crush her. You don't even have to compete—you just keep doing you."

Bethany grinned in spite of herself. "Yeah, I will. I am going to crush Marigold by pretending she doesn't exist."

Chapter 2

"What are you serving today?" Olive asked.

Bethany stirred the huge stock pot. "Split pea with smoked ham hock. Seemed perfect for such a foggy day."

"What'd be good with that? Maybe my cornbread muffins...or a cheddar biscuit."

"Can't go wrong with either one if you ask me. Uh oh—here comes trouble."

Even though she'd sworn to pretend Marigold didn't exist, it was impossible to ignore her. Bethany tried not to stare as Marigold swept through the entrance doors. She wore her usual skintight wiggle dress and red, patent-leather heels, but something about her seemed different. She held the door open for another woman who was pulling a red wagon loaded down with two giant pots.

"Oh my goodness!" Olive gasped. "She didn't!"

"Morning, ladies," Marigold said. "What do you think?"

"About what? The wagon?" Bethany asked.

Olive groaned. "About her *hair*. It's...new."

"Oh!" Bethany took a closer look. Marigold's white-blonde curls had been dyed a lustrous auburn and were arranged in a messy bun on top of her head. "It looks—like mine."

"Exactly!" Marigold squealed. "Isn't it great? Soup sisters for life!"

At least until your roots grow out.

"Is that your actual sister?" Bethany asked, nodding to the woman pulling the wagon up the kiosk, who was puffing with the effort. She looked remarkably like Marigold—at least, Marigold before she dyed her hair. She had the same blonde hair, the same voluptuous figure, and the same glitzy style. The only difference in their appearance was the prominent beauty mark on the woman's upper lip. Marigold penciled one on, or sometimes glued a small gem in the same spot, but it was obvious that this woman's was real.

"Oh. No." Marigold pursed her lips. "Cousin Jen. Surprise visit."

The cousin blushed and extended her hand.

"We hug around here." Olive ignored Jen's hand and embraced her. "I'm Olive—I own the bakery. Welcome to Newbridge. How long are you staying?"

"That's up to her." Jen motioned to Marigold and shook Bethany's hand across the kiosk counter.

Bethany did her best to smile. "Must be nice for you two to catch up." Jen nodded shyly. *Hm, however much she looked like Marigold, she certainly had a different personality!*

"She's going to be my assistant for the grand opening," Marigold said. "There's so much to do! Why don't you put that soup on the warmer? We don't want it to get cold, do we?" Jen nodded and slowly dragged the heavy wagon over to the Souperior Soups kiosk.

Marigold shook her head. "She's been stuck to me like glue since she came in yesterday. Crashed the poker game even though she didn't want to play. Wouldn't even have a martini. What a party pooper."

Bethany's ears perked up at the mention of the poker game. "Oh, did Ben talk to you last night?"

"Of course he did. All Ben does is talk, talk, talk. 'Marry me, Marigold.' Who has time for that? Marriage, shmarriage."

Olive and Bethany exchanged a look that said one thing: *poor Ben.*

"He didn't mention anything about changing your kiosk?" Olive asked.

Marigold stuck out her chin. "No—not that it's any of your business. Why are you over here, anyway? Shouldn't you be baking or something?"

"She was just helping me with bread pairings," Bethany said.

"Ooh!" Marigold leaned on the counter. "What would you pair with avgolemono? That's my soup of the day."

Bethany choked. Olive patted her on the back until she regained her composure. "You mean like I made yesterday?"

Marigold nodded eagerly. "Mhm. It was a tasty little number—perfect for my grand opening! Everyone loved it, so I know they'll be back for more."

"Well!" Olive said, smoothing her silver bob. "Everything I make has gluten in it, so I don't think I can help you."

"What about your—" Bethany had been about to say *gluten-free dinner rolls*, but Olive shot her such a steely glare that she stopped in the middle of her sentence.

Marigold waved her hand breezily. "No worries. I bought a case of saltines at Cheapko. I'll just serve those." The clock tower chimed a quarter-till, and Marigold straightened. "Oopsie, I better get things set up before the 10:55 comes in! Toodles!" She minced off to her kiosk.

If ever a tea kettle was steamed up and ready to shout, it was Olive Underwood. "Unbelievable! Un-be-lievable. The nerve of copying your recipe and serving it with *crackers*!" Bethany returned the favor and patted her on the back until Olive turned a less volcanic shade of red.

"Soup of the day," Bethany said, rolling her eyes. "More like soup of the yesterday."

"Poor Jen." Olive frowned. "To be related to *that* woman. She's treating her own cousin like garbage."

Bethany sighed and wrote "Split Pea with Ham" on her chalkboard. "Do you think my regulars will choose Marigold's soup instead of mine?"

"No, of course not! Don't even think that way. Your customers love what you do. Why would they gamble on someone else when they know they'll love every drop of your soup? Uh oh! There's the train. I better get those cheddar biscuits warming." Olive scampered back into the Honor Roll just in time. A flood of passengers exited the platform, and Bethany's heart swelled when a good number of them lined up at Souperb Soups.

"Here you are." She ladled soup into a container and handed it over the counter. "Olive's got cheddar biscuits and corn muffins today if you want something on the side."

"Perfect, Bethany."

"Smells great."

"Mmm."

"I haven't had a good split pea soup since my grandma passed."

"Can I get the recipe?"

Bethany basked in the glow of satisfied customers. Nourishing people's hearts and stomachs had to be the best feeling in the world. Her pot was half-empty and the line was still long.

Maybe there was enough room for two soup kiosks at New-bridge Station after all. She glanced over at Marigold's kiosk. A few people she didn't recognize milled around the booth.

"Avgolemonooooo," Marigold called, her hands to her mouth. "Get it here!"

Bethany was horrified to see a few people from her line step out and hurry to the other booth. Her dismay must have showed on her face, because the kindly man at the front of the line said, "Oh, everyone's in a hurry these days. Your soup is worth a few minutes' wait."

"Thanks," she said, relaxing. That was it. She just needed to serve faster. The defectors would get a bowlful of disappointment and be back tomorrow, anyway. She put down her head and ladled soup as quickly as she could so she could get through as many customers as possible.

"I brought you some, hon." Marigold plunked a container of soup down on the counter. "Wanted to soup-swap before you ran out again."

"Who is serving at your—oh," Bethany said, spotting Jen at the counter. She bit her lip. If she gave some split pea soup to Marigold, Marigold would probably just copy it tomorrow. But if she didn't honor the trade, Marigold was likely to make a scene, and the customers waiting patiently in line didn't need to see that. She slid a bowl of soup over to Marigold. "Take it."

Marigold leaned over the bowl and inhaled deeply. "Smoked ham! Nice. Are those carrots in there or sweet potatoes?"

"Carrots." Bethany craned her neck to see the next person in line. Marigold didn't budge. Instead, she scooped up a spoonful of the soup and savored it like she was tasting wine.

Bethany sighed. "Do you mind, Marigold? I need to serve the rest of these people."

"Not until you try mine!" Marigold tapped the lid of the unopened container with her spoon.

"Fine." Bethany cracked open the avgolemono and took a small bite, not expecting much. *Rich, bright, comforting.* It was a perfect replica of the soup she'd made yesterday, down to the hint of marjoram. Marigold might not have her own ideas, but she was a darn good cook.

"What do you think?" Marigold pretended to bite her long purple fingernails in anticipation.

"I can't lie—it's good."

Marigold squealed and danced in place. "Victoryyy! I mean...yours is good, too."

"OK, I've got customers," Bethany said pointedly. Marigold twirled around a few more times and capered off to her kiosk.

"Friend of yours?" the next customer in line asked, as Bethany ladled out a container of split pea soup.

"Not really. Why?"

"Just curious." The man set another container on the counter. He took out a small notebook and jotted something down, and then put it back into the pocket of his denim shirt.

"That'll be three dollars."

As the man pulled out his wallet to pay, Bethany noticed that the container he'd put down on the counter was from Marigold's kiosk. "Hedging your bets, huh?"

He handed her the three dollars. "No—I'm here from the paper."

"Come again?"

"The newspaper. I write the Sunday food feature for the *Newbridge Community Observer*. Milo Armstrong," he added, adjusting his thick-framed glasses. "I probably should have introduced myself first."

Milo Armstrong was pretty cute. Behind his geeky glasses, he had warm eyes in a delicious chocolate shade and an even warmer smile.

"What brings you here, Mr. Armstrong?" she asked, her stomach fluttering nervously. She hoped it wasn't a follow-up on last year's debacle. She'd had enough of *that* kind of coverage in the *Community Observer*. But maybe her little kiosk had finally made enough of a name for itself that they were sending a food reporter to write about her soups!

"Milo," he said, flashing that smile at her again. "Ms. Wonder invited me down to compare the two soup kiosks at the station for this week's feature, kind of a head-to-head thing."

Any bubble of hope that had buoyed her spirits immediately popped. As much as she wanted a food feature, a surprise cooking competition was *not* cute. "I wouldn't have made split pea if I'd known!" she burst out without thinking.

"Oh?" He raised an eyebrow and pulled out his notebook again. "Why's that?"

"Well, split pea soup is comforting, but it can be a bit stodgy," she babbled nervously. "Some people don't like it because of bad childhood experiences. It's not what you make to win a contest."

"Are you sure you're not just saying that because you're afraid of the competition? I had a bite of her soup already, and it's exceptional."

"Why, thank you!"

He eyed her skeptically. "I haven't tasted yours yet—I was talking about Ms. Wonder's."

"I know. I made that avgolemono yesterday." Bethany crossed her arms.

"Are you saying she stole your recipe?" Milo's pen was poised over his notebook, ready to record her response.

"No. Well, sort of. She ate some of my soup yesterday, and what she made today is exactly like it. And it's tough for split pea to compete with that—it was one of my best soups ever. What are you writing?" Bethany stood on tiptoe to peer at what he was scribbling, but she couldn't decipher his handwriting upside down.

"Just some notes." His brow furrowed. "I'm curious—if you made one of your best soups yesterday, why not make it again today? Why make something that you know is worse?"

Bethany sighed. "It's hard to explain. I make soup to fit the day: the mood, the atmosphere, the weather, whatever. This morning it was foggy, so split pea seemed like a natural choice. Plus, I never cook the same soup twice—or I try not to. I make soup of the day, not soup of the yesterday. I'm kind of regretting it now, though."

"Aw," Milo said, his eyes twinkling with amusement. "I promise you a fair and unbiased review. I'm not here to make anybody look bad."

How could she explain that she'd put her life savings into Souperb Soups and worked her butt off for the last nine months, and Marigold had put in *one day* and a new sign, without sounding peevish? *Hmph*. "It's not exactly a fair review, though, is it? Because she knew you were coming and I didn't. If you really wanted to be fair, you'd come back another day—one we *both* know about."

He tapped his finger to his lips, considering. "OK. You've convinced me. I'll give the tasting another shot tomorrow, and that way you'll both be prepared. You can serve up your best, whatever that may be."

Bethany snorted. "Well, I know what Marigold will be cooking—split pea with smoked ham. Soup of the yesterday."

Milo chuckled. "Then I guess I won't bother with this, since I'll be having it tomorrow." He pushed the container of soup back across the counter. Bethany started rummaging in the till to retrieve his three dollars, but he held up his hand. "No, no, keep it, Ms.—?" He broke off questioningly.

"Bradstreet. Bethany Bradstreet."

He nodded. "Right. See you tomorrow, Ms. Bradstreet." He turned on his heel and sauntered off to Marigold's kiosk, whistling.

Who *whistles* anymore? Bethany shook her head and swept the container of uneaten soup in the trash. As she cleaned up the kiosk for the day, she reflected that she should have at least had the guy *try* the split pea. If he didn't come back tomorrow, she might have missed her last chance at getting a review in the newspaper...plus, to be honest, she kind of wanted to see that warm smile again.

• • • •

"I THINK I MIGHT HAVE blown it." Bethany wrapped her hands around her mug of hot chocolate and peppermint whipped cream.

"Aw, no, honey, you didn't! You set yourself up for success!" Kimmy sat down at the kitchen table and slurped the topping off her own mug. "If he'd tasted the soup, he still could have written that head-to-head article without your permission. At least this way, it's a level playing field. Don't get me wrong—your split pea is great! But it can't compete with that avgolemono."

"I know," Bethany said glumly. "I can't believe Marigold was able to recreate it so exactly. She's going to do this to me every day from now on, isn't she? No matter how good I am, she'll just match me. And pretty soon, people are going to start going to her first."

"Stop saying that!" Kimmy slammed her fist on the table, causing the spoons to rattle in their mugs. "And stop selling it to her!"

"Can I even do that? Legally?"

"Of course you can! It's your product—you can sell it to whoever you want! You can be like the Oprah of soup." Kimmy put on her best Oprah impression. "You get a soup! You get a soup! You *don't* get a soup."

Bethany snorted into her hot chocolate. "You're saying I should be the anti-Oprah?"

"No, I'm saying even Oprah would not be giving soup to this lady. Marigold is ripping you off. She can cook and she has good taste buds; girl don't need to be lazy. If you stop *literally* feeding her your recipes, she'll just have to succeed or fail on her own merits."

"I guess I can start by not giving it to her for free. That way she's at least paying to use my recipe."

Kimmy bounced her fist on the table again. "That's right! Now you're talking."

Bethany glanced at the clock. Almost midnight. "Now I better figure out what I'm going to cook for that reporter."

"Hey, all you have to compete with is split pea, right?" Kimmy grinned.

Bethany shook her head. "I can't count on it. Marigold is full of surprises—she might just make avgolemono again. I need to bring my A-game. What do you think about minestrone?"

Kimmy wrinkled her nose. "Kinda basic. It's like the pumpkin spice of soups. How about vichyssoise?"

"I don't even know how to spell that."

"OK, carrot ginger? Nice bright flavor, easy to spell…"

Bethany hemmed and hawed. "Nah, I think that's too simple. Only one texture. I want something with a little heartiness, but a light broth with a lot of aromatics." She drummed her fingers on the table. "Like maybe the most epic chicken noodle ever."

"Oooh! I like that. I like it a lot."

"Does that mean you'll let me have the keys to Café Sabine so I can work on my stock all night?" Bethany clasped her hands together pleadingly.

Kimmy chewed her lower lip, looking torn.

"Just this once? It's only for the food review, and I'll owe you big time. I'll do anything you want—I'll cater your wedding when you marry Charley!"

"Seems a little premature, considering Charley and I have only been dating for four months, but I am going to hold you to that."

"Is that a yes?" Bethany grinned hopefully.

Kimmy nodded. "But I'm going with you. Monsieur Adrien would kill me for giving you the keys, but if I'm there getting work done, too, he can't really argue. And you better cook the soup of your life if I'm going to stay up all night."

"This is going to be just like when we were in culinary school and we'd stay up all night cooking together!"

Kimmy smiled. "Those were the good old days. Slumber party in the kitchen. I'm down this once, but let's not make a habit of it."

"Deal." Bethany held out her pinky, and Kimmy linked fingers with her.

"Deal."

Chapter 3

Bethany stifled a yawn as she wheeled Daisy through the door of the station. The lid on the stock pot jostled, emitting fragrant steam. Bethany closed her eyes and breathed in deeply. *Herbal, full-bodied, hint of spice.* It was sure to impress that reporter with the warm brown eyes and the Clark Kent glasses—what was his name?

She opened her eyes and narrowly avoided crashing Daisy into Ben and Trevor, who seemed to be arguing.

"I don't care—it's unacceptable!" Ben poked his finger into Trevor's chest. "We can't afford—"

"Sorry, guys!" she said. "I just need to get set up." They stepped aside, resuming their discussion in more hushed tones, and she pushed Daisy over to the Souperb Soups kiosk. She put the soup on the warmer and wrote "Epic Chicken Noodle" on her chalk board.

"Meow!"

Bethany peered over the counter. Caboose sat at attention in front of the kiosk, flicking his tail. Apparently he thought the soup smelled good, too. "Sorry, sir, I'm not open until eleven. If you're hungry, you'll have to go catch a mouse." She shooed him away; even one stray cat hair could mean a bad review in the paper. He stalked off toward the bakery, his tail straight and indignant.

She couldn't help herself, then—she sneaked a look over at Marigold's booth to see what her soup of the day was. Jen was there, busy stirring a vat of thick, green liquid.

"Did she copy again?" Olive asked, leaning to peek around the counter at Marigold's kiosk, too.

"Yep, split pea." Bethany tried not to feel too smug. After all, the reporter hadn't tasted either soup yet, and maybe he didn't like chicken. Maybe he didn't like soup that he had to chew. Maybe—*oh, who am I kidding? I've got this thing in the bag.* "Here, have a taste and tell me what you think for the bread pairing."

Olive sipped the spoonful of soup that Bethany offered and closed her eyes blissfully. "Wow. Normally I'd say maybe an onion roll to liven up chicken soup, but I'm not sure with this one—it's so flavorful. It needs a bread to stand up to it but not compete. Plain, old-fashioned sourdough?"

Bethany nodded. "I could see that, or maybe a brioche to sop up—" she broke off as she watched Trevor storm to Marigold's kiosk. He seemed to be angry about something, and poor Jen looked terrified.

"What's he so mad about?" Olive whispered. Bethany shrugged. Trevor raised his voice, but Bethany couldn't make out what he was saying. Jen shrank back from the counter, her hands behind her back like she was searching for an escape route. Bethany held her breath—would Trevor step into the kiosk to menace Jen even further? He yelled at Jen again, leaning across the counter and gesturing wildly. When Trevor whirled and left in a huff in the direction of the maintenance room, she finally exhaled.

"Wow, I've never seen him like that! He's usually so chill." Bethany shook her head in disbelief. "Poor Jen."

Olive nodded. "I know! Maybe it's just the stress getting to him. His wife is pregnant—their first—and the baby is due this week. That's enough to send any man over the edge."

"You'd think he'd get used to the idea after nine months. I wonder if he's just passing along the negativity from Ben. I saw Ben yelling at him about something when I came in. I know Trevor's having a hard time keeping up with the maintenance on the station, but it's not really his fault—this place needs a lot of work."

"Well, whatever the reason he blew his stack, Jen doesn't deserve it," Olive declared. "I'm going to go see if she's OK before Marigold shows up."

"Talk to you later." Bethany stifled a yawn.

Olive stopped short. "What's up with you? That's the fourth yawn in a row. You can hardly keep your eyes open."

"I was up all night working on my chicken stock. I hope I can make it through the lunch rush without falling asleep with my head on the counter!"

"I'll get you some coffee in a minute," Olive promised. She left to fuss over Jen. A few minutes later, she brought Bethany an enormous latte from the bakery, the foam decorated with a cocoa swirl.

"Thanks, Olive. You always take such good care of me." Bethany smiled at her and downed as much of the hot coffee as she could. It'd be great if her eyelids were open when the reporter showed up.

"Anything for you, dear."

Bethany leaned against the counter and dozed off for a minute, letting the caffeine do its work, but her eyes flew open when she heard the clock tower chime 10:45. The coffee had made its way to her bladder, and she *really* had to go. With only ten minutes left before the train came in, she couldn't wait. She'd have no chance later, when she had customers lined up.

"Marigold, can you watch my—" Bethany looked over and saw Marigold still wasn't at her kiosk, and now Jen was gone, too. The split pea soup simmered on the warmer, but no one was behind the counter. She walked quickly over to the bakery and stuck her head through the door.

"Keep an eye on my till while I run to the ladies' room?"

Olive nodded, waving a floury hand. Bethany hustled down the concourse, walking as quickly as she could past the ticket booth and maintenance room toward the restrooms. Just as she reached the door to the ladies' room, she saw Jen opening the door to the men's. Caboose prowled in the hallway nearby.

"Is the ladies' full?" Bethany asked.

Jen shook her head. "Um, it's"—she winced—"clogged or something." She slipped into the men's room and closed the door, clearly as anxious as Bethany to get back to the kiosks in time for the lunch rush. Bethany waited, tapping her foot impatiently. Caboose yowled and pawed at the door to the maintenance closet across from the restrooms. Two minutes passed, then three. She couldn't wait any longer. She dashed back down the concourse, through the main doors, and across the street to Café Sabine.

She went through the back entrance and stuck her head into the kitchen. "Hey Kimmy! Can I use your restroom? The train station's is clogged." Kimmy nodded, sliding a tray of *vol au vents* from the oven, and Bethany ducked into the small restroom that was only used by the kitchen staff.

She made it back to Souperb Soups just in time. She heard the 10:55 train pull in, but there was no rush of passengers exiting the platform. *Strange*. She didn't have long to think about it, though, because the newspaper reporter, Milo, strolled up to her counter and slapped down his notebook.

"I hope that look of puzzlement isn't because you forgot I was coming, Ms. Bradstreet." He grinned mischievously.

She felt her cheeks turn pink. "Forget you? No way—I made something to blow your mind." Bethany pointed to the chalk board.

"Epic chicken noodle," he read aloud. "Sounds promising. I wonder what Ms. Wonder came up with to compete."

"Take a wild guess."

"Soup of the yesterday?" He winked at her.

"Oh, so you're funny *and* smart."

Ack, that was flirting! What if he thought she was trying to butter him up to give her a good review? Bethany died a little inside. "Uh...I mean...just kidding. I'm sure you're normal...average. Whatever." Bethany flushed beet red—this was only getting worse.

Milo seemed intent on ignoring her awkwardness. "How about that soup?"

Bethany gratefully turned to the stock pot and was ladling out a bowlful of epicness when she heard a loud commotion. People were yelling and running from the platform.

"Someone got hit by the train!" a man shouted. The swinging doors to the front entrance smashed against the wall as a pair of paramedics ran in carrying a stretcher, followed by a couple of police officers.

"Everybody stay in the building," one of the cops announced through a bullhorn. "I repeat—remain in the train station until an officer takes your statement. This is a crime scene."

"Are they really going to lock the whole place down?" Milo asked.

Bethany nodded, her heart banging in her chest. "They must suspect foul play if they're calling it a crime scene. I guess we're stuck here until they can figure out what happened."

"I'm so sorry," Milo said. "I really have to go."

"You can't leave! The cops just said we have to stay here."

He shook his head. "If nobody can come in or out of the station, that means I'm the only reporter with access. I have to call my editor and tell him we have the scoop! No offense, but the food feature isn't exactly front page news."

"'No offense.' Why does that always precede something really offensive?"

"I'll make it up to you?" He smiled apologetically and stuffed his notebook back into his jacket. "I have to go cover this—a good crime story could be my big break! I'll come back later to try the soup, I promise." He tapped the counter with his fingers like he was playing a set of tiny drums. "Wish I could stay—I really do, but..." He pointed at her and then left without finishing the thought.

Bethany sighed. It was petty to think that her soup was more important than someone getting hit by a train, but she couldn't help being a little disappointed. She glumly stuck a spoon in the bowl that should have been Milo's and ate it herself. The taste perked her right up. The broth had the perfect balance of richness and brightness, the handmade noodles were perfectly cooked, the vegetables were crisp-tender, the organic chicken was abundant. A tiny *ping* of cayenne and the freshness of parsley rounded out the flavor. She closed her eyes—it was a winning soup.

"You open?" a customer asked.

Bethany opened her eyes and nodded. The passengers from the 10:55 were milling around the concourse, looking a bit lost now that they had been kicked out of the platform area by the cops. Might as well serve them lunch. "Sure am."

"I'll take a bowl. Looks like we're stuck here until they can get through talking to everyone."

"Did you see what happened?" Bethany snapped the lid on the container of soup.

The man shook his head. "I felt the operator slam on the brakes, but I guess it was too late. Sad, really."

"Someone jumped in front of the train?"

"I don't think so. I overheard someone say the conductor was shaken up because he saw a person push the lady. That's the rumor, anyway."

"Thanks for filling me in."

"No problem. Can I get bread with this?"

Bethany pointed him to the Honor Roll and moved to serve the next person in line. It made her stomach hurt to think about someone intentionally pushing another person in front of the train, especially right here in Newbridge Station. *Who would do something like that?* She hoped it was just an accident.

As Bethany served her chicken noodle soup, more and more of the 10:55 passengers noticed their fellow travelers eating and came over for their own bowl of soup. Even Marigold's kiosk was bustling—it seemed like Jen was working her fingers to the bone getting out that split pea with ham, her cousin nowhere in sight. It figured that Marigold would stick the poor woman with all the hard labor.

Bethany stirred the stock pot, already down to the dregs. It'd probably be gone by the time Milo came back. *That figured, too*.

"Hey, Bethany. How're you doing?" Charley asked, her face unusually serious. Her detective badge was pinned to her navy-blue blazer, and she was clearly on duty.

"OK, I guess—soup's pretty much gone, though—sorry. It was a popular one."

"I'm not here for lunch. I'm here about Marigold."

Bethany groaned. "What has she done now?"

"Hon, she's dead. She's the one who was hit by the train." Charley looked at her sympathetically. "I'm sorry to be the one to tell you."

Bethany felt the blood drain from her face. "Oh god. That's terrible."

"Do you have any contact information for her next of kin? We didn't find her purse, so we're not sure who to call."

Bethany racked her brain. "Um, I don't know her family. We weren't really friends. Oh, wait—her cousin Jen is visiting! She's over there, working in Marigold's kiosk. She'll know." Bethany motioned to where Jen was serving soup, and was surprised to see another person standing next to her behind the counter—a bearded man she didn't recognize, wearing a snap-back hat that said "I've Been Better."

"Wait here while I notify the relatives," Charley said grimly. "I need to ask you some questions."

Chapter 4

Wednesday afternoon

Bethany watched as Charley walked over to Marigold's kiosk. She could tell her friend dreaded giving the bad news, and Jen didn't take it well. She was so shaken that she leaned on the bearded man for support. He looked strained, his face tense and unhappy, as he rubbed Jen's shoulders to comfort her. Must be a boyfriend or husband.

I should do something for Jen, the poor woman, Bethany thought. But what? Maybe Olive would have an idea; she was great at that stuff. Bethany realized that Olive might not know what had happened to Marigold. She glanced over at Charley, who was still asking Jen questions. Of course, she had to take statements from everyone. It would only take a minute to run into the bakery and update Olive on what had happened. Charley probably wouldn't even notice she was gone.

Bethany slipped into the Honor Roll. A nod to Olive's former career as a history teacher, the bakery was school-themed. The walls were white with blue horizontal lines to resemble notebook paper, and the legs of all the chairs were painted to look like number-two pencils. The walls were hung with pull-down maps, and every table had a deck of trivia flashcards so bakery patrons could test their history facts. Even the baked goods were inspired by the classroom—on the menu were A+ Pastries, Top of the Class Breads, and Dean's List Desserts.

To her surprise, Olive wasn't there. Instead of Olive's neat silver bob and warm smile greeting her, a bald old man wearing a plaid shirt and suspenders glowered behind the counter as he bagged baked goods and made sandwiches. Olive's husband, Garrett, a retired carpenter, helped out at the bakery when Olive was short-handed. Usually he was building shelves or fixing a broken table, but sometimes he got roped into running the register.

"Hi." Bethany smiled. "Is Olive around?"

"Errands," he grunted.

"When do you think she'll be back?"

Garrett shrugged. His face looked drawn—maybe he'd heard about Marigold. "Not soon enough."

"OK, thanks—I guess I'll talk to her later." *Weird that Olive was running errands during the lunch rush.* Bethany hadn't seen her leave, so she must have left while Bethany was using the restroom at Café Sabine—but why would she go somewhere when she was supposed to be keeping an eye on Bethany's kiosk? It wasn't like her to flake on something like that, but maybe she'd delegated the task to Garrett. Bethany shook her head. It didn't matter now; nothing had been taken from her booth.

When she got back to her kiosk, Charley was standing there, drumming her fingers on the countertop. "I told you to stay put! Where'd you go?"

"Into the bakery to tell Olive about Marigold." Bethany shrugged apologetically.

"Just because I'm your friend doesn't mean you can ignore my instructions. This is a murder investigation, Bethany! When you disobey me, it makes you look bad, and things already aren't great for you."

Bethany's mouth fell open. "What do you mean? Do you think I had something to do with it?"

Charley sighed. "Everyone knows you were upset about her serving soup at her kiosk."

"Not upset enough to push her in front of a train!"

Charley tapped her clipboard. "Let's take a step back. Where were you just before the 10:55 train came in?"

"In the restroom," Bethany answered automatically.

Charley clicked her pen a few times and didn't write anything down. "You sure about that?"

"Of course I'm sure! Olive brought me a huge coffee this morning because I was exhausted from cooking all night, and my bladder wouldn't have made it through the lunch rush, so I went to the restroom before the train came in."

"OK, we have a problem, then, because Jen says *she* was in the bathroom, and you say *you* were in the bathroom, and there's only one toilet in the ladies' room. So you wanna tell me how you were both peeing in the same pot?"

Bethany let out a sigh of relief. "Oh, yeah. The ladies' room was out of order. I saw Jen going into the men's room, but I didn't have time to wait for her to come out. I went over to Café Sabine and used the kitchen restroom—you can ask Kimmy."

"I will." Charley jotted down some notes. "What'd you do after you left the café?"

"Um, came back here to serve lunch. I heard the 10:55 train pull in right after I got back, and then the food reporter showed up to taste my soup."

"Was he writing a review?"

Bethany nodded. "Marigold called him to do a food feature comparing our two kiosks. It was kind of a surprise."

"And how did you feel about that? Were you upset?"

Bethany gaped at Charley. "No! I mean, yes, but not murder-level upset. I thought it was unfair that I didn't know about the competition when the reporter showed up yesterday, but I was glad for the chance to have my food reviewed, so I asked him to come back today so I could prepare a better soup. He agreed."

"What's his name? I'll need to talk to him to verify your story."

"Milo Armstrong, I think."

Charley rolled her eyes. "Oh, *that* guy. He's been following us around and asking annoying questions all day. I'll check with this Armstrong guy and Kimmy about your alibi, Bethany, but don't go anywhere, OK? Until we clear you, it's important that you stay in the station. And think about anyone you might know who had a beef with Marigold."

"Yes, officer!" Bethany mock-saluted, grinning, and Charley rolled her eyes.

As Charley walked away from her kiosk, Bethany felt her throat tighten. How could her friend think she was capable of hurting someone like that? She didn't want Marigold to *die*, she just wanted her to go back to making smoothies or something—anything—other than soup. Of course, now the whole head-to-head food feature was pretty pointless, so Milo wouldn't be back for a tasting. Leave it to Marigold to mess up people's lives even after she was dead. Bethany angrily brushed the tears from her eyes. Maybe she had a pinch of ill will toward Marigold, after all.

Just then, she noticed Olive rushing toward the bakery, looking every bit like a ruffled hen. Bethany stepped out to meet her. "What's wrong? Are you OK?"

Olive waved her hand. "Oh, these police officers. Wouldn't let me through the doors because of some issue on the tracks. I told them the Honor Roll is my livelihood, and it has nothing to do with the trains. They can't keep me out of my own bakery."

"And they let you through?" Bethany asked. She admired Olive's gumption standing up to the cops.

"Well, I might have promised them some free brownies if they let me in," Olive said guiltily.

Bethany chuckled, and then remembered why the police were there to begin with. "Olive, the problem on the tracks—someone was pushed in front of the train."

Olive gasped. "That's terrible!"

"It's worse. It was Marigold."

Olive's eyes widened. "Marigold pushed someone? Who?!"

Bethany shook her head. "No, she was the one killed."

"What?! Why would someone *do* that?"

"Charley said they didn't find her purse, so I'm thinking maybe it was a robbery."

"Oh dear," Olive said, her eyes welling up. "That's unexpected."

"I know. I was thinking we should do something for Jen. She must be devastated."

Olive's hands fluttered to her cheeks. "Oh, yes, we must. What do you think? Cupcakes? I made some I'm calling 'Homecoming Queen' because they have the fluffiest frosting and edible glitter on top, and you know Marigold loves glitter. Loved," Olive corrected.

"Perfect. A little sweetness and sympathy will go a long way."

While Olive fetched the cupcakes, Bethany finished closing up the kiosk. Clearly, Milo wasn't going to show, and the soup was gone, anyway. She'd have to wash up the pots at Café Sabine later, once the police released the scene.

Strange to think that all the worrying about her business she'd done over the last couple of days was for nothing. Though Souperb no longer had direct competition, now there'd be no food feature. No chance to shake off the past and show Newbridge who she really was. No chance to see Milo Armstrong again, either. She sighed.

"Here," Olive said breathlessly. "I picked white, because the pink ones seemed too happy. What do you think?"

"Good. They're over there on the bench." Bethany watched the bearded man holding Jen, his chin on top of her head, while she cried into the sleeve of her pearl-buttoned cardigan.

Olive clucked sympathetically as they walked together over to the bench.

"Jen? I brought you cupcakes—we did. I just want you to know how sorry we are."

Bethany nodded in agreement. "Is there anything we can do? Do you have a place to stay?"

Jen sobbed, and the bearded man spoke for her. "The police told us to stay away from the apartment. We have a hotel for tonight."

Bethany couldn't quash her curiosity about the man who seemed to have appeared from nowhere. "And you are?"

"Aaron. I'm her fiancé. I just came in on the 10:55, the one that...well. It's very upsetting, as you can imagine." He spoke quickly in a low voice, his fingers stroking Jen's hair.

Jen lifted her face, streaked with mascara-black tears. "She was meeting the train. It's so awful—it's my fault she was down there. It should have been me."

Aaron shook his head. "No, it's my fault. I should have canceled my interview in New York and just come with you on Monday. If I had been here, she wouldn't have been on the platform, and this wouldn't have happened."

Olive looked on the verge of tears again herself. "Oh, you poor dears. It's not your fault. It's the fault of whoever did such a horrible thing."

Jen smiled wanly.

"Do you know of anyone who had a grudge against Marigold?" *Besides me*, Bethany silently finished. "Maybe someone who was upset with her? Did she talk about being scared or worried or anything?"

Jen shook her head. "I haven't visited her in a while, and we're not very close. I only really know what I've seen since I've been here, and it's not like she introduced me to her enemies. I met a couple of her friends—but now that I think about it, the friends she does have aren't happy with her. One of the guys she plays poker with even yelled at me this morning."

Bethany looked at Olive. They'd both seen Trevor blow his top at Jen. "What was he upset about?"

"He said she borrowed his keys, and he wanted them back. I didn't have them. He wanted to know where she was, so I told him."

"Where was she?"

"She went to the bank. She was going to meet the 10:55 train on the way back to pick up Aaron, but when I told Trevor that, he freaked out. I thought he was going to hit me or something. He said he needed his keys to do his job and that she was going to get him fired." Jen looked at the floor and more tears seeped down her cheeks. "What could I do? I just told him I was sorry and asked if anyone else had a set of the keys he could borrow. Then he stormed off."

Aaron stiffened and squeezed Jen more tightly. "He had no right to treat you that way. No right."

Olive nodded. "That was out of line even if it were true."

Aaron stood up. "What do you mean *if* it were true? Are you calling my fiancée a liar?"

"Oh, no!" Olive waved her hands apologetically. "I meant that I don't think Trevor would loan Marigold his keys. If she wanted a door opened at the station, he'd just unlock it for her. He needs the keys to do his maintenance rounds. Twice a day, he has to check all the systems in the tunnels, make sure the track is clear, and so on."

Aaron crossed his arms and raised his eyebrows skeptically. "Well, I guess he's dumb enough to loan them out when a pretty woman asks him."

"I don't know if it's true"—Jen tugged Aaron's hand so he'd sit back down on the bench—"but that's what he said. Maybe you could ask him about it."

Bethany nodded. "I'm sure there's a logical explanation. In the meantime, is there anything we can do for you to help you out?"

Jen looked over at Marigold's kiosk, where the pots of split pea soup were still simmering on the warmer. "I have no idea what to do about the booth. There's a ton of soup left."

"Don't you worry about a thing," Olive said, patting Jen on the shoulder. "Bethany and I will take care of it. I'll run the soup down to the shelter where I donate my day-old bread, and she'll have the kiosk closed up in a jiffy."

"Fine," Aaron snapped. "It's none of our business, anyway. We just want to go home and leave this nightmare behind us."

"Sorry," Jen said. "It's been such a terrible morning."

"Don't apologize," Bethany said. "It's very upsetting. Hopefully the police will let everyone leave soon, and you can go to your hotel and relax."

"Yes, let us know if you need anything. And don't forget your cupcakes!" Olive put the bakery box down on the bench next to Jen. As they left the couple to close up Marigold's kiosk, Bethany looked down the concourse to see if Trevor was among the crowd, but there was no sign of him.

"Why would Trevor give Marigold his keys?" she wondered aloud.

"I don't know that he did," Olive said darkly. "You know he guards those keys with his life. Maybe she took them."

"Oh, just because she's annoying doesn't mean she's a thief."

Olive snorted and pointed to the split pea soup still simmering on the warmer. "What are you talking about? She *is* a thief! She stole your recipes—and your hair color, for that matter!"

Bethany rolled her eyes. "I don't own this hair color. You're missing the point. Whether Trevor loaned her the keys or she took them, he was angry with her about it. The question is—was he angry enough to push her in front of a train?"

Olive squawked indignantly. "Of course he didn't! He wouldn't do something like that."

"Well, we've never seen him that angry before either, have we? And that was *at Jen*, who wasn't even involved. Imagine how he'd have acted if he was confronting Marigold. It could get ugly, fast."

"I don't even want to think about that," Olive said, shaking her head. "Oh, dear, lunch is almost over. How am I going to take these pots to the shelter if the police won't let us out the door!"

"It'll keep on the warmer. I'll close up, and we'll just have to remember to take the soup later when the police release the scene. The shelter can serve it for dinner."

"Good idea, Bethany—that way I can relieve poor Garrett, too. You know he hates working the counter." Olive tutted and went back to the Honor Roll.

Bethany stirred the split pea soup to make sure it wasn't scorching and closed the lid tightly. She wiped down the counters, organized the condiments and cutlery, mopped the floor, and stowed the "Open" sign. As she drew the canvas curtains around the kiosk, she looked up at the Souperior Soups sign Marigold had installed. She glanced around—Jen and Aaron were intently engaged in conversation, and none of the 10:55 passengers were in the immediate vicinity. No one would notice if she took down the sign. It would need to come down anyway, so why not now?

She grabbed the stepladder from under the counter and set it up, then rummaged around in Marigold's shoebox marked "tools." No screwdrivers, only nail files and a kit for repairing stocking runs. Bethany sighed and went to look in her own toolbox. No luck there, either—she only had a flathead screwdriver to adjust the heat on her warmer, and the screws in the sign needed a Phillips head. Her shoulders sagged; the sign would have to come down another day.

As she was folding the stepladder, she noticed Trevor at the other end of the concourse, walking toward the maintenance closet. He would definitely have the right kind of screwdriver, and borrowing it would be the perfect opportunity to ask him about why he loaned Marigold his keys.

She jogged over to the maintenance closet and cracked open the door. "Trevor? Got a minute?"

"Uh, sure."

Bethany pushed the door all the way open. The maintenance closet was long and narrow, lined with shelves full of bins and boxes. At a workbench on the far end, Trevor was untangling a mess of wires. "I wondered if I could borrow a Phillips screwdriver?"

"What's broken now?" Trevor grumbled.

"Well, the women's restroom is clogged, but that's not why I need the screwdriver. I just want to take down a sign."

"If it's a station sign, you'll have to get approval from Ben," Trevor said. "He's like Emperor Palpatine—he twitches a finger, and everyone has to do what he says."

"Well, he is the boss. I take it you're not happy with him right now?"

Trevor put down the tangle of wires and exhaled. "No, I'm not happy. He wants me to do twice the work, but he won't pay for overtime hours. Then he gets on my case because *his* girlfriend wants special favors. I'm just trying to do my job around here, but I can't win!"

Bethany remembered almost crashing into the two of them that morning. "Is that why Ben was yelling at you today?"

Trevor nodded. "I was trying to get those dang emergency sprinklers fixed before the fire department shuts us down, and she needed to get into Ben's office because she left her purse in there last night, so I let her borrow my keys for a minute. I figured he wouldn't mind since they have a thing going on, but when he found out, he blew his stack at me."

"But she didn't just borrow them for a minute, did she?" At his surprised expression, Bethany shrugged apologetically. "Jen said that you were upset because Marigold hadn't returned the keys."

Trevor sputtered. "I needed them to do my rounds. I can't access the maintenance tunnels without them."

"Totally understandable that you'd be annoyed." Bethany nodded. "You were doing her a favor, and then she was taking advantage of you."

"Exactly!" Trevor brightened. "It's so nice to talk to someone who understands."

"Can I ask you something?" Bethany said in a conspiratorial tone. "Where were you when Marigold got hit by the train? Did you see it happen?"

Trevor shook his head and looked a little green around the gills. "I was in the tunnels—I didn't see anything. What kind of screwdriver did you need, again?"

"Phillips."

"Here." He handed her a screwdriver. "That ought to do the trick. Don't blame me if Ben comes down on you, though—I'll say I didn't know anything about it. Oh, and put an out-of-order note on the restroom door so other people don't use it. I'll get to it when I can, but I can't make any promises about when that'll be. Just use the men's and remember to lock the door."

"OK. Thanks, Trevor." Bethany stepped back into the hall. She started toward the concourse, but then remembered she needed to put a note on the bathroom door. And, now that Trevor mentioned it, maybe she *should* tell Ben that she planned to take down the Souperior Soups sign. She doubted he'd object to the sign's removal, but he might object if she did it without asking.

She walked the other direction down the hall, past the maintenance closet and restrooms, to the stationmaster's office. The door was open, and Bethany could see Ben at his desk using an old adding machine, the kind that printed a long paper tape. As she watched, he ripped off the tape, crumpled it up, and threw it on the floor.

"Everything OK?" she asked cautiously from the doorway.

"Fine, fine. I just can't make the numbers work."

"For what?"

Ben rubbed his forehead. "The restoration fund. We just don't have enough to keep up with repairs, and a systems upgrade is out of the question. At this rate we'll have to close within a year."

"Can ZamRail just *close* a station?"

"Oh, sure. People would have to use Oldbridge Station instead. Drive over the bridge, or take the bus if they don't have a car." Ben leaned back in his chair and stared at the ceiling. "ZamRail would sell the building, and it'd become a craft brewery named The Station or something. That's what happens to all these old buildings."

"Wow, I had no idea." Bethany sat down across the desk from Ben. "I was just talking to Trevor about how he's not getting overtime, but I had no idea it was because the budget was so tight."

Ben nodded, his forehead creased with worry. "It's only going to get worse now that Marigold was killed. All the bad publicity. Fewer people will use the station, fewer people will donate to the restoration fund...it's all downhill from here. I doubt anyone will want to take over Marigold's kiosk now that its former tenant was murdered, so the station will lose that rent, too."

"How long can the station stay open?" Bethany mentally tallied up her bank account—a big fat zero. The revenue from Souperb paid her bills, but just barely. If the station closed even temporarily, she'd be in trouble.

"Without a windfall? One month, maybe two before the maintenance will completely drain the budget. The place needs a complete overhaul. A disaster like this is the last thing I need." Ben closed his eyes, his fist pressed against his mouth.

"I'm so sorry about your girlfriend." Bethany bit her lip. "You must be in shock."

"She wasn't my girlfriend," Ben said quickly, straightening. "We didn't have a relationship."

"But she said—" She'd forgotten that Ben had proposed to Marigold.

"Marigold said a lot of things, mostly to make herself look good." Ben wore a surly expression. "We were friends. We played poker once a week. That's it. Wait, why did you come here? Do you want something?"

"I wanted to ask you about taking down the Souperior Soups sign now that Marigold's kiosk is closed. Trevor said I should ask your permission."

"Probably because he doesn't want to do the work. I swear, that guy is the laziest—"

"No worries there!" Bethany waved the screwdriver. "I'll do it."

"Fine." He turned his attention back to the adding machine.

Bethany started to leave, but then her curiosity got the better of her. "Just one more question...I remember you were doing the maintenance rounds earlier in the week? Did you do them this morning, or did Trevor?"

Ben looked up from his paperwork. "He did. I've been doing *this* glorious task all day."

"Does he follow a checklist, or does he do the maintenance in any order he wants?"

"A checklist, why?"

"I was just wondering what he would have been doing when the 10:55 train came in."

Ben frowned thoughtfully. "A track check is the last step, right before the train arrives."

"So Trevor is possibly the last person to have seen Marigold alive?"

"I imagine so. He would have been on the platform just before the train arrived. He's supposed to stay on the platform until the train pulls in, actually."

Bethany debated how much of her conversation with Trevor she should reveal to Ben. She didn't want to get him in trouble, but just the same, she didn't want to pin a murder on him by omission, either! If she let Ben think that Trevor was on the platform when Marigold was killed, he might tell the police, and Trevor could get in trouble. "He said he was in the tunnels when the train came."

Ben nodded and didn't seem surprised. "That wouldn't be unusual. If the track was clear and he saw the light change because the train was coming in, it's likely he'd just go back through the maintenance tunnels to work on another project. He's got plenty to keep him busy."

"Sounds like it," Bethany said. "Speaking of, can I borrow a piece of paper and a pen? The ladies' room is out of order, and I want to put a note on the door."

Ben pushed a sheet of paper across the desk to her and pointed at a pen set, before turning his attention back to his adding machine and list of figures. Bethany hastily scribbled "Out of Order — Use Men's Room" on the paper. "Before I go..." she began hesitantly.

"What?" Ben's irritation showed in his voice.

"I was just wondering if Marigold's purse was here in your office. The police said it wasn't with her, and Trevor said that she'd left it in here last night. I thought if it was here, her cousin might like to have it back. I could take it to her."

"I don't have it."

"Do you know where it is?"

"I said I don't!" Ben's voice was so loud he was nearly shouting. "Close the door on your way out."

Bethany jumped and skittered out of the office, slapped the out-of-order notice on the women's restroom, and knocked on the door to the maintenance closet again. "Trevor? You in there?"

No answer. She pressed her ear to the door. She could hear someone inside rummaging through boxes. She knocked again, louder. The door flew open, and Trevor's face emerged, red and sweaty with the effort of whatever he was doing.

"You again. What do you want now?"

"I talked to Ben, and—"

Trevor rolled his eyes and slammed the door in her face. The noise inside resumed, and this time it sounded like Trevor was dumping boxes of metal pieces out on the floor. *What in the world can he be doing?* Bethany knocked again, pounding with her fist until he cracked open the door.

"What?"

"I wanted to know if you saw Marigold when you did the track check at the end of your rounds this morning."

"No, I didn't. I already told you I didn't see anything."

Bethany stuck her foot in the door so he couldn't close it again. "You said you didn't see the train hit her. I'm talking about before that, when she was just standing on the platform. You might have been the last person to see her alive."

"So? She was standing on the platform. I didn't push her in front of that train."

"I wasn't accusing you of anything. I was just curious if anyone was with her. If you saw Marigold, you probably saw the murderer, too."

"I don't know. I was checking the tracks, not making a list of everybody I saw."

Bethany nodded. "Well, if you remember anything..."

"I'll tell the *police*," Trevor said pointedly. He started to close the door again, and Bethany tried to see around him to the interior of the maintenance closet.

"What are you doing in there, anyway? It's awfully noisy."

"Looking for something. It's none of your business." He scooted her foot out of the way with his own and closed the door again. This time, she heard it lock.

What could he be looking for? The maintenance closet was cluttered but well-organized, with labeled boxes and bins for parts and tools. He shouldn't have to dump everything out on the floor to find an item. She'd never seen him act so agitated about anything, either. What was stressing him out so much? Could it be something to do with Marigold's death?

Bethany shook her head to clear it. *Don't be so suspicious all the time!* He probably just misplaced a small part and figured it fell down into another box or something. Or maybe he was just frazzled because of his impending fatherhood. She walked back across the concourse to her kiosk and was surprised to see the waiting area nearly empty of passengers. The police had obviously released the scene. Jen and Aaron weren't on the bench, either—they must have gone to their hotel.

Bethany took a deep breath and exhaled slowly. The morning's caffeine had worn off, and had been nearly thirty hours since Bethany had slept. Her eyes felt gritty, but she shook off the exhaustion and climbed the stepladder to take down Marigold's sign. The leggings and tunic she wore didn't have pockets, so she held the screws in her lips as she removed them. One end of the sign was free, and she held it up with one hand while she leaned to reach the last screw on the other side, causing the stepladder to wobble.

"Be careful up there, hon!" Olive stared up at Bethany. "You have a minute to take the soup over to the shelter with me?"

"Mhm," Bethany mumbled through a mouthful of screws. Holding the sign, she backed down the ladder, spat the screws into a container, and slid the sign under the counter of Marigold's kiosk. *Well, not Marigold's anymore.* Her death still didn't seem real. She peeked under the lid of the soup on the warmer. "I'm a little worried about the temp on this. I'm afraid it'll cool too much on the ride over. Is it OK with you if I turn up the heat, and we wait a few?"

Olive hesitated, but then nodded. "Fine. Come get me when it's ready."

Bethany turned up the warmer and headed back to Souperb, where a coating of chicken stock was hardening on her own pot and ladles. She piled the utensils into the stockpot and carried them over to Café Sabine.

When she pushed through the swinging doors to the kitchen, she saw Kimmy's back through the door to the walk-in refrigerator.

"Hey!" she called, and Kimmy jumped and turned.

"You surprised me! You're late."

Bethany plunked the stockpot into the deep dishwashing sink, squirted some dish liquid into it, and turned on the hot water. "Police were holding the scene until they interviewed everyone. It was a mess."

Kimmy closed the walk-in and grabbed some disinfecting spray from under the sink. As she began wiping down the counters, she said, "Charley told me about what happened. So sorry."

"She checked with you about my alibi?"

Kimmy paused mid-spray. "Yes! And I chewed her out for badgering you. I can't believe she questioned you like that."

"Don't be mad at Charley; it's not her fault. She's just doing her job."

"I don't have to approve, though," Kimmy grumbled. "I can't believe she'd even consider you a suspect, especially after all you went through last May."

Bethany nodded and attacked the inside of the stock pot with a scrubber. She didn't want to think *or* talk about last May. Cleaning was somehow more satisfying than usual, and she scrubbed even harder at the remains of the epic chicken noodle soup until the stainless-steel pot shone.

"Soup was a hit?" Kimmy asked.

Bethany nodded, keeping her eyes trained on the dishwater.

"What did the reporter think?"

Bethany shrugged, and Kimmy shrieked in frustration. "Come on! Give me something, here. I did not stay up all night with you to be ignored in my own kitchen!" Then she softened. "Sorry. I didn't mean to blow up at you. I'm just tired."

"Me, too," Bethany admitted. "Anyway, he didn't taste the soup."

"What?!" Kimmy stared at her, the spray bottle slack at her side.

"He was standing there, about to have some, right when we found out Marigold got hit. He left my kiosk to cover that story for the paper since the station was locked down and no other reporter had access. It doesn't matter now, though, does it? With Marigold out of the picture, the food feature is a nonstarter."

Kimmy nodded. "With the competition dead, the competition's literally dead."

"Morbid way to put it, but yeah." Bethany rinsed her pot and ladles and then dunked them in the sanitizing bath. "And I am honestly disappointed. I know I complained about the food feature because it was a surprise, but it was my shot, you know? It was finally some attention that wasn't about Daniel's murder."

"You mean some attention from a guy who isn't Daniel." Kimmy eyed her slyly.

"Milo's a professional, and he was only there to do his job. I'm sure I'll never see him again." Bethany blushed in spite of herself. "That's not why I'm disappointed, anyway. Well, not the *only* reason."

"It's about time, is all I'm saying. You deserve to have a little fun."

"I have fun!" Bethany said indignantly.

"Mhm. Name one Saturday in the last three months that you've gone out."

"I stay home on purpose. I love hanging out with you and Charley. And I ride my bike—that's fun. And I read."

"Super fun." Kimmy's smirk was visible across the room.

"I don't need a boyfriend to enjoy my life."

Kimmy cackled. "So get a girlfriend!"

"Can't—all the good ones are taken. Guess I'm stuck being single." Bethany smirked at her friend. If she was honest with herself, it would be nice to see Milo again without the strange pressure of a food review. Maybe she'd run into him somewhere else...the waterfront, maybe? Or just walking down the street. She wondered if he'd recognize her outside the kiosk, or if he only saw her as fodder for another newspaper article. Kimmy yawned and Bethany's mind snapped out of her daydream. "What time is it? I have to get back to help Olive."

"Go. Shoo," Kimmy said, motioning for her to leave. "I'll finish putting this stuff away."

Bethany trudged over to the station and waved to Olive through the bakery window, pointing to the door questioningly. Olive saw her and waved her inside. Bethany helped her carry Marigold's leftover soup out to her car, a green station wagon that was nearly the same color as the split peas.

"We have to make it snappy. I left Garrett at the register again." Even Olive looked tired after today's events.

"He's not a fan of dealing with customers, is he?" Bethany settled into the passenger seat and closed the door as Olive started the car.

"He doesn't mind that so much." Olive nosed the car out of the parking lot and headed downtown. "He's just put in a lot of time today already, and he's not feeling great these days."

These days. Meaning it wasn't just a passing cold virus. "Is something wrong? Is he OK?"

Olive kept her eyes trained on the road. It was Newbridge's equivalent of rush hour, and while the town never backed up with traffic the way New Haven did at this time of day, enough cars were on the street that driving seemed to capture her full attention. "He'll be fine."

She was usually so chatty and open. Why wasn't she explaining Garrett's health situation—was she hiding something? *It's probably just something embarrassing like hemorrhoids*, Bethany chastised herself. Still... "Is that why you were gone today during the lunch rush?"

"Yes and no."

"What were you up to? Garrett said you had errands, but usually you run your errands later in the day."

Olive pulled the car into the small lot behind the homeless shelter. "Here we are." She practically jumped out of the car, leaving Bethany to wonder if she was just eager to get back to Garrett or if she was avoiding the question. *Maybe she's just not ready to talk about it, yet.* It could be something serious—Alzheimer's, maybe.

She scrambled out of the car and helped Olive carry the soup into the building. They entered through a low doorway into a sterile, tiled hallway.

"This way," Olive said, turning to the left, and Bethany followed her into a large kitchen. Everything in it, from the floor to the countertops, was white, and rows of gleaming steel utensils and pots and pans hung from hooks on the walls. The air was filled with the smell of chickens roasting in the massive pair of ovens.

Bethany stopped and marveled at the space. "Wow, I wish I had a kitchen like this."

"The kitchen at the café is lovely!" Olive said. "On three. One, two..."

They hefted the stock pot onto the range, and Bethany clicked the knob until the burner came on, then turned it down to the lowest flame. "It's great, but Café Sabine isn't my kitchen. I'm just lucky Kimmy works there and doesn't mind me taking up space during her prep."

A woman poked her head out of a doorway Bethany hadn't noticed. "I couldn't help overhearing. If you want to cook here, we'd love to have you. We can always use more volunteers!" She emerged from the room—the pantry, Bethany realized—lugging a ten-pound sack of rice.

"Hi, Sister Bernadette," Olive said, smiling. "We had a big pot of leftover soup at the station, and I thought you might be able to use it."

"We made sure it stayed at temp," Bethany added.

Sister Bernadette clasped her hands. "Wonderful! I take it you're the soup genius Olive is always talking about?"

Bethany looked at Olive. "I guess so. This isn't mine, though."

"Well, it's one of your recipes," Olive said wryly.

"Either way, we are happy to have it. And I'm not joking about you cooking here. We could use someone with expertise to help with menu planning, too, so we're eating more seasonally and wasting less food. Come see the rest of the place." Sister Bernadette, a fiftyish woman with plain features and graying hair swooped into a low bun, didn't seem prepared to take no for an answer.

"Olive really has to get back," Bethany protested as the sister herded them into the dining room across the hall from the kitchen. If Garrett was experiencing dementia or another serious illness, she was sure Olive would be anxious to return.

"Don't be silly, we can take a few minutes," Olive said, her face smooth and unconcerned.

Maybe Garrett just had arthritis or an ingrown toenail, Bethany mused. But if his health problem wasn't serious, why wouldn't Olive have waited until after the lunch rush to run her errand? Even a couple of hours later would have been a better time to leave the bakery. Maybe the "errand" wasn't about Garrett's health at all. She quashed her suspicions and gave her full attention to Sister Bernadette as she showed them around the dining room.

"We set the dining room up like a restaurant. Our guests order from a short menu—just two entrée choices, usually. It gives them some dignity to sit down at tables with real table-cloths instead of standing in line." Sister Bernadette smiled at a trio of women who were setting the tables for the evening meal. "Some of the guests work as wait staff, but we're mostly volunteers. Oh, Ryan!" Sister Bernadette called to a man walking by in the hall. "We'll have to add bowls to the tables tonight. Olive's friend brought soup!"

"Really?" The man came into the dining room. Tall, with dark olive skin and brilliant green eyes, the man had one of those inscrutable ethnicities. His hair was twisted into short dreadlocks and his T-shirt clung to his fit frame, making Bethany rethink her whole "abs are gross" thing. He stuck out his hand. "Hi. I'm Ryan, but I guess you know that."

Bethany took his hand automatically and a jolt of electricity zipped up her arm that nearly took her breath away. "Bethany," she said. "I have a soup kiosk down at Newbridge Station. It's not my soup, though. I mean, what we brought." Her face flushed, and Olive gave her a smug look.

"I'm sorry to hear about what happened at the station to-day. You must be shaken." Ryan still hadn't let go of Bethany's hand.

"We're all right," Bethany said, glancing at Olive, who avoided her eye contact. "Happy for a distraction, though."

Ryan finally dropped her hand. "Did Sister Bernadette in-vite you to volunteer? We're desperate for another chef in the kitchen, especially on Saturday nights."

Bethany could hardly look away from his magnetic gaze. *Was this guy a volunteer or a shelter guest?* Paint-splattered jeans, sneakers with holes in the toes...he wasn't dressed like a professional doing charity work. "Uh, yes, she did."

"So will you?" He looked eager and unselfconscious, like he didn't know he was the most gorgeous thing on two legs.

"Please do," Sister Bernadette said, gently touching Bethany's elbow. "Think of it as a chance to try out new recipes on a very enthusiastic audience."

"And to cook something other than soup!" Olive said. "You need to keep your skills sharp if you're going to open that restaurant someday."

Bethany put up her hands and laughed. "OK! I give up—I can't resist all three of you. I'd love to help out."

"Wonderful, just wonderful!" Sister Bernadette exclaimed. A wide smile lit her face. "Ryan, why don't you finish the tour while Olive and I get bowls on the tables? Show Bethany what you've been working on."

"We have to go," Bethany protested, thinking of Garrett glowering behind the bakery counter. "The Honor Roll is still open and—"

Olive shook her head, winking at Bethany. "Nonsense. We have plenty of time."

"It's pointless to argue with these two," Ryan said cheerfully. "Come on."

Bethany resigned herself to the tour—it was clear she wasn't getting out of it—and followed him down the hall. She looked back over her shoulder and Olive gave her a thumbs-up. Her cheeks burned, and she could hear Olive giggling as she and Ryan rounded the corner.

He pushed open a door. "This is the business center. It has laptops with internet access, phones, office supplies, cameras, a printer—"

"So people can apply for jobs?"

Ryan nodded. "Yeah, jobs, but also fill out forms for housing, do taxes, run businesses, write papers for classes, all kinds of stuff. We're really lucky to have it here."

"Business owners and college students live in a homeless shelter?" Bethany asked. Ryan's brow furrowed, and she immediately regretted the question.

"Stereotypes are dangerous. All kinds of people live here." His face seemed to harden a little as he closed the door and moved down the hall.

"I'm sorry," Bethany said, hurrying to keep up with his pace. "I just couldn't tell if you were speaking hypothetically or if people really use the business center in the ways you describe."

"We do." Whatever ease and unselfconsciousness he'd had in the dining room fell away, and even his posture seemed stiffer and more formal.

Bethany winced. So he was a guest at the shelter, and she'd basically just insulted him. "That's great," she said, trying to salvage something from the conversation. "Really great."

Ryan's voice was flat as he pointed out other rooms. "In there are the storage lockers for people's stuff and a big wardrobe of professional clothes to borrow. In that one we have kennels for pets. Mostly dogs, but some other animals, too. Bedrooms are upstairs." He led her to the end of the hall and into an expansive room furnished much like a nice hotel lobby, with comfortable sofas and armchairs. Several people were relaxing there, reading, chatting, and playing board games on the gleaming tables. "This is the common area."

"How nice!" Bethany exclaimed. "This is somewhere I wouldn't mind hanging out."

"Not what you were expecting from a homeless shelter?" He coolly raised an eyebrow.

"Honestly, no. I thought it'd feel more...I don't know. Sad. I'm sorry if that sounds ignorant, but it's the truth."

Ryan's shoulders relaxed and the corners of his mouth quirked up. "I'm going to give you a break and just say that I'm glad you got to see what it's really like. Sister Bernadette and volunteers like Olive work hard to make sure this is a place of hope, not despair. But I had the same assumptions as you when I first came here. I think most people probably do."

"Well, I'm glad you forgive me." Bethany smiled warmly at him. She didn't know what Ryan's deal was, but she hoped that the shelter would help him find stable housing and get his life back together. He seemed like a really thoughtful guy—someone she might date if he weren't homeless. The instant she had the idea, she mentally chastised herself for stereotyping again. His housing situation was just temporary circumstances, not a sign of bad character. *Still.* "So what have you been working on? Sister Bernadette said you should show me."

"Ah!" His face lit up. "Turn around and you'll see."

Bethany turned and saw, behind where they'd been standing, an enormous mural that stretched the length of the common room's back wall. It was a landscape—two villages separated by sapphire-blue ocean, with a bridge between them and a glowing sunset in the hills beyond. *That explained the paint-splattered jeans.* "It's Oldbridge and Newbridge!" she exclaimed. "You're an artist?"

Ryan nodded proudly. "Still putting on the finishing touches. See here?" He touched a Victorian house on the Newbridge side where a tiny figure was planting flowers in a garden. "I'm working on the little stuff."

Bethany moved in closer to get a better look at the details. She spotted Café Sabine and the train station, the marina and the park, the public library and town hall, each painted with painstaking accuracy. "You have every business—maybe every house. And so many people doing different things. Commuters on the train, children at school...I love the fishing boats out on the harbor, too! I can even see the fish they're trying to catch under the waves." She turned to him in awe. "This must have taken months!"

"Well, weeks, but yeah." He couldn't keep the grin off his face. "I wanted it to be beautiful from any vantage point. You know, some people take a big view, some people can only see what's right in front of their noses. I hope this will remind viewers to try the opposite way of seeing sometimes, too."

Bethany nodded. "So this is what you do for work? Paint murals?"

Ryan shoved his hands in his pockets. "Well, it's what I like to do—I don't get paid."

Bethany felt a pang of sympathy, remembering how painful it had been when she was unemployed in the months before she opened Souperb Soups. If Kimmy hadn't fronted her the rent during that time, she could have easily found herself without a place to live. "Well, it's obvious you're a hard worker, judging by all the things they have you doing around here. I'm sure you'll find a job. Actually, I bet there are a lot of local business-es that would love to have murals like this. Maybe even some of the city buildings."

"You think?"

Bethany nodded. "You have real talent, Ryan. And it seems like the business center here has all the tools you need to get something off the ground."

"I'll think about it," he said, shrugging. "I kind of like doing it for free. I'm not sure it'd be the same to paint for hire."

Well, that attitude explained why he'd been living at the shelter for weeks. "I guess that's your choice," she said.

"Don't get me wrong—I appreciate the encouragement." Ryan smiled at her, and his smile was so charming that she couldn't help returning it. "I've just tried the whole working-for-a-boss thing, and it didn't turn out great for me."

"Me neither," she admitted. "That's why I started my soup kiosk. It's not big, and it's not fancy, but it's enough to pay my rent, and I get to do what I love every day."

"Right, but you aren't a personal chef. You get to decide what you paint—I mean, cook."

"For better or for worse. People don't always eat it."

Ryan raised an eyebrow. "That's not what I've heard. Olive says you're a magician, so I'm looking forward to finally getting a taste on Saturday."

Something about his wording and playful tone made her blush. Why was this guy having such an effect on her? She shook her head.

His face fell. "You're not going to come?"

"No, I am. I just don't want your expectations to be too high. It's just soup." *And you're totally inappropriate for me, so I have to stop flirting with you.*

Ugh, maybe that was the underlying appeal—the absolute horror her parents would experience if they knew she was even thinking about what it'd be like to date a homeless guy. Bad enough that their daughter turned down the scholarship to Yale and wasted her mind on culinary school. They were still telling their friends that she was planning to go to law school. She wondered sometimes if all her impulses were just simple rebellion against their expectations.

No, that wasn't true—she genuinely loved cooking. And surely her parents would see her ambition and achievement once her dream of owning her own café came to fruition, wouldn't they? *Pipe dream—they'll never get it.* Just like they'd never see Ryan's talent and work ethic; they'd only see a homeless guy.

"If something nourishes and comforts people on a deep level, it's not 'just soup.'" Ryan touched her shoulder gently. "Don't diminish what you do."

Tears suddenly welled in her eyes, and she felt a knot of sadness creep into her throat. "Why do you understand what I do without even knowing me?"

He shrugged. "The artist in me recognizes the artist in you."

Chills ran down her spine. She stared at him, her eyes pricking with tears. "Who *are* you?"

He chuckled uncomfortably. "Just another human being. Come on—I'll get you back to Olive."

Shaking her head, she followed him back down the hall to the dining room, where Olive was setting flower arrangements on the tables. Bethany could hear a timer going off in the kitchen, and Sister Bernadette apologized as she scurried to check on it.

"Almost time for service!" she chirped on her way out. "See you Saturday!"

"You'd better get busy," Olive admonished Ryan.

"Yes, ma'am."

"And come by tomorrow afternoon to pick up some bread." Olive winked at Bethany, who rolled her eyes. Olive's attempts to push them together were so transparent, and frankly, unwelcome. The rollercoaster of emotions she'd been on today was too much, and frankly, she wanted off this ride.

"Bye," she said firmly.

"Don't forget what I said." Ryan looked at her steadily. "You're an artist."

She nodded and pulled Olive out the door. Someone like Ryan, who valued art over everything—even having a home—couldn't really understand her, either. It was time to go sleep off the confusing fog of fear, regret, suspicion, and self-doubt that had been swirling around her. Tomorrow *had* to be a better day.

Chapter 5

Thursday morning

When Bethany woke, she knew exactly which soup to make to counteract Wednesday's mess. The day required something invigorating, something that represented renewal—and New England oyster season was in full swing. Spicy tomato and oyster stew was the perfect solution. The pressure of the food feature off her shoulders, she truly enjoyed the morning prep at Café Sabine—making fish stock, chopping herbs, opening the shellfish.

"I've never seen someone so happy to shuck oysters," Kimmy said.

"You don't fully appreciate a good night's sleep until you skip one." Bethany breathed in the smell of the stew: *briny, spicy, enticing*. She'd add the oysters in at the last minute and then it'd be heaven in a bowl.

"Tell me about it." Kimmy rolled her eyes. "I was up longer than you were. At least you got to go home after you served lunch. That reminds me, are you doing OK with the whole Marigold situation? Be honest."

Bethany sprinkled a tiny bit of Old Bay seasoning into the stew. "Do you think Olive could bake oyster crackers to pair with this? Would that be asking too much?"

"Crackers don't take very long. I'm sure she could whip some up." Kimmy paused. "Hey, you're avoiding my question!"

Bethany nodded. "I don't really want to think about it. I mean, it's not like Marigold and I were friends, but that almost makes it worse. If I'd known she was going to die, I'd have been nicer to her."

"Well, we're all going to die at some point."

Bethany grinned. "Are you saying I should be nicer to everyone?"

Kimmy nudged Bethany with her elbow. "Can't hurt."

"I don't know, it sounds pretty painful to me!" Bethany's words were joking, but her heart felt heavy in her chest. "Actually, it's making me a little paranoid. I see pretty much every person who goes in and out of Newbridge Station. What if the killer is one of my regulars? Any bowl of soup I serve might be eaten by Marigold's murderer."

"Murderers gotta eat, too."

Bethany nodded. "Murder is hungry work. Takes a lot of calories."

Kimmy cracked up. "You're sick!"

"You started it. Anyway, this is one of those 'if you don't laugh, you cry' situations. I don't want to think it's anybody I know, but everyone is acting weird—myself included. I feel like everyone's a suspect."

"Not *everyone*. Not, like, Olive."

Bethany said, "Well..."

"No!" Kimmy stuck out her bottom lip. "You can't be serious."

"She really didn't like Marigold. That whole gluten thing was personal. *And* she wasn't at the bakery at the time of the murder."

"Stop. Just stop right now. You gotta turn off the suspicion faucet and let Charley do her job. Otherwise you're going to get my middle school social studies teacher arrested. She's a nice little old lady, not a killer!"

"I just don't like to rule out possibilities," Bethany said stubbornly. *Not that Olive did it, but I can't say she* didn't, *either.*

Kimmy stamped her foot. "That's it, get out of my kitchen!" She grinned and added, "It's coming up on 10:30."

"OK, OK." Bethany slid the shucked oysters into the stew and strained their liquor to the pot for good measure. "I'm done here, anyway."

When she wheeled Daisy into Newbridge Station with her steaming pot of spicy oyster stew, for a moment she forgot that anything out of the ordinary had happened yesterday. She steeled herself for Marigold's inevitable jabs, but when she looked up, it wasn't Marigold barreling toward her—it was Olive.

Olive reached out with both hands and gripped Bethany's forearms. "Be careful, sweetheart," she said. Before Bethany could ask what she was talking about, Olive rushed back to the Honor Roll.

Bethany shook her head. *What was that all about?* Was it a warning? A threat? She glanced over at Marigold's kiosk. It was closed, shrouded in canvas like a piece of old furniture. So it was all real—Marigold was dead, and someone killed her. Bethany shivered.

Be careful, sweetheart. Olive's words echoed in her head as she went to unload the cargo trailer. To her surprise, a customer was already waiting at the counter. Well, maybe not a customer—it was Milo Armstrong, culinary critic for the *Newbridge Community Observer*, with Caboose sniffing at his shoes. What was he doing there? Had Olive been warning about him?

"Souperb opens at eleven," Bethany said as she put the soup on the warmer. "I'm surprised to see you, though, now that the food feature is dead in its tracks." She grimaced. *Poor choice of words, Bethany.*

"I'm not wearing my food critic hat today." He tugged the brim of his baseball hat as Caboose purred and wound around his legs. "If I can pull off a good story this week, my editor said he'll let me work the crime beat more often."

"That hat *is* a crime," she said, and winked at him.

"This your cat?" Milo eyed Caboose distrustfully.

Bethany shook her head. "Nope, he just works here. Ol' Caboose shows up to beg for soup, but he's supposed to prefer rodents." She wrote "Spicy Oyster Stew" on the chalk board. Milo wrinkled his nose. "Not a fan of seafood?"

"Not a fan of spicy."

Bethany's jaw dropped. "How can you be a food critic if you don't eat spicy stuff? That's like half the world's cuisines."

Milo shrugged. "I can't help it—I'm a supertaster. I have the gene that makes flavors more intense, especially chilies. It's actually an asset as a food professional. Quite a few professional chefs are supertasters."

"Seems like a liability to me," Bethany muttered. "Anyway, the stew isn't that spicy. Just a little to balance the richness of the oysters."

"You just might talk me into it." Milo smiled, his warm brown eyes trained on hers. Caboose pawed at his leg for attention until Milo reached down and gave him a good head-scratching.

Bethany leaned over the counter to watch the cat luxuriate in the attention. "I think he likes you."

"I think he's hoping for my leftovers." Milo grinned, but then rearranged his face into a more serious expression. "Can I ask you about what happened yesterday? You know everybody involved."

"Involved?" She frowned. *Nobody I know was involved—were they?*

"You know, the regulars at the station: employees, passengers, bakery patrons, and so on. People like Marigold. I remember you said you weren't exactly friends."

"We weren't."

"Why not? You were in the same business, spent a lot of time together. Shared ideas. Seems like a natural friendship."

Bethany narrowed her eyes. She remembered that conversation with Milo. She had told him that Marigold copied her soup, not that she'd shared ideas with her. "I think you need to do some fact-checking."

"Why, am I off base?" He widened his eyes and flipped back through his notebook. Bethany couldn't tell if he truly didn't remember the content of their conversation, or if he was baiting her into airing grievances against Marigold. Well, she wasn't going to take the bait, no matter how much he batted his lashes.

"Marigold and I didn't spend much time together. We were too busy helping customers. She only recently switched from serving smoothies to making soup, so we hadn't really been in the same business until the last few days." The minute the words slipped out of her mouth, she regretted them.

Milo jumped on it, as she knew he would. "So you were angry when she changed her business model." A statement, not a question. Caboose pawed at his leg again, but Milo didn't even look down at the cat, just shook his pant leg until Caboose lost interest and sat a few feet away, licking his paws and washing his face. *Maybe the cat-lover shtick was just that—an act.*

Bethany shrugged. "It wasn't my favorite thing ever, no. But I wasn't out-of-control mad or anything. I went to talk to Ben—"

"The stationmaster?" Milo interrupted, scribbling in his notebook.

Bethany nodded. "To ask him to talk her out of it. He said he would, but he didn't. Or he did and it didn't work."

"So you complained, and nothing happened. She continued to sell soup. Did it bother you that she was getting special treatment because she was Ben Kovac's girlfriend?"

"She wasn't his girlfriend," Bethany said automatically, but then second-guessed herself. Why did she say that? Marigold herself had said Ben *proposed*, for goodness' sake. And Trevor said they had a "thing." Only Ben had denied they were in a relationship. *Why didn't he want to admit to a relationship with Marigold?*

"That's not what I heard," Milo said, tapping his notebook with his pen. "I'd have been pretty mad. Might have taken matters into my own hands. Maybe you confronted her and got into a tussle, and she went off the edge of the platform by accident."

Bethany rolled her eyes. "Are you serious? You were literally at my kiosk two minutes after the train came in. Unless I can teleport, there's no way I could have pushed Marigold onto the tracks and made it back to my booth while the train was still pulling into the station."

Milo tilted his head as though he were sizing her up. "I don't know. Someone who knows the station well, blends in, doesn't draw suspicion...I think you could have made it back in time."

This could not be happening. The only dateable guy in New-bridge, who also happened to be a food critic, thought she was a murderer. Bethany looked around to see if someone—*any-one*—around could come dig her out of this hole. She was grateful to see Charley coming through the main entrance, the perfect person to set Milo straight.

"Charley! Charley!" Bethany waved her hand so Charley would notice her. Charley saw her and smiled, jogging the rest of the way over to the Souperb kiosk. The sudden movement made Caboose dart along the wall toward the stationmaster's office and out of sight.

"What's up?" Charley leaned on the counter and looked Milo up and down. "This guy bothering you?"

"No, but could you please tell him I'm not a murderer?"

Charley laughed. "She has an alibi, dude. We checked it out. Go bark up another tree."

Milo touched his notebook to the brim of his baseball cap. "Sure thing, Detective Perez." He walked a few feet away and paused, scribbling furiously in his notebook.

"What're you doing here, anyway?" Bethany asked, turning away from Milo.

"Follow-up on the Marigold Wonder case. Came to ask around about some things the coroner found on her body. I guess I can start with you, since you're here."

"OK, shoot. I have a couple more minutes before the 10:55 rolls in." Bethany gave the stew a stir. Out of the corner of her eye, she saw Milo sidle closer to them to better hear their conversation. She jerked her head toward him so Charley was aware of his presence.

Charley made a face. "Shoo," she said to Milo, who grudgingly took a few steps back. She turned her attention back to Bethany. "Any idea where Marigold would get a big fat check?"

Bethany frowned. "Like how big are we talking?"

"Fifty Gs. Cashier's check."

"What? No way! I thought you didn't find her purse."

Charley nodded. "We didn't. It was in her bra along with her cousin's social security card."

"Do you think someone killed her because they wanted to steal the check? That'd explain why her purse was gone. The killer probably assumed the check was in there."

"I can't speculate on an ongoing investigation—you know that." Charley stood up straight, as if she'd just realized she was there as a police detective and not as a friend of Bethany's. "So, any reason you know of that she'd have that much money? Recent inheritance, sell a car or home, switch banks, something like that?"

Bethany shook her head. "I don't have any idea. Although...Jen said Marigold was going to the bank yesterday morning."

"Which bank issued the check?" Milo craned his neck over Charley's shoulder, trying to get a glimpse of her clipboard. "Oldbridge Federal. Thanks!" He took off for the exit. *And once again, any chance at a food feature—or a date—runs out the door.*

"Argh!" Charley glared at his back and couldn't keep the disgust out of her voice. "*Reporters.*"

"Sorry. I feel like it's my fault he was here."

"Nah, forget about it. They're all vultures." Charley smiled sympathetically.

"Speak of the devil!"

Charley furrowed her brow, confused. "Vultures?"

"No, Jen. Look!" Bethany pointed over to the ticket window, where Jen and Aaron stood in line. They each had a carry-on suitcase with them. "I think they're leaving Newbridge."

"Lucky you saw them. Ms. Smith! Mr. Andrews!" Charley raised her arm like she was hailing a cab. Jen and Aaron looked over and then looked back at the ticket booth. "This will just take a moment." They glanced at each other and then reluctantly grabbed their suitcases and wheeled them over to where Charley and Bethany stood.

"Where are you headed?" Bethany asked.

Aaron rolled his eyes. "We're not on vacation here. We're going home."

"To make funeral arrangements," Jen added, her face drawn.

"I just have a couple of follow-up questions," Charley said. "I won't keep you long, but this is important. Do you know why Marigold might be carrying a large sum of money? Family inheritance or something? We found a check on her body."

Jen gasped. "You did? No, I don't know why she'd have money. Her bank account was virtually empty as far as I knew."

"Is that all?" Aaron tapped his foot impatiently. "If we don't get our tickets in the next five minutes, we'll have to wait an hour for the next train."

Charley held up her finger. "One more thing. Along with the check, Marigold also had Ms. Smith's social security card—I can return that to you now." She flipped up the first couple of sheets on her clipboard until she came to a plastic baggie. She slid the baggie out and presented it to Jen, who accepted it with two fingers.

"Thanks." Jen opened her purse and dropped the card inside, still encased in the plastic bag.

Bethany gasped. "That's Marigold's handbag!" She'd recognize that brand of tacky anywhere.

Jen clutched it to her side. "It's mine!"

"Look, Charley, it says 'M.W.' in rhinestones, Marigold's initials. I know it's hers because I noticed it when she was buying soup from me on Monday. That's definitely Marigold's purse, the one that's missing from the crime scene."

"She left it in the kiosk," Jen said, covering the monogram with her hands.

Bethany narrowed her eyes. "You said she went to the bank. Why would she go to the bank without her purse?"

Charley stepped between the two women. "Bethany, can you please leave the questioning to me? You're interfering with this investigation!"

"For your information, she gave it to me! We swapped. She said we'd be handbag sisters." Jen sniffled and pulled a tissue out of the handbag to dab her nose. "If a purse is missing, it'd be mine. Black, patent-leather, vintage Chanel."

Suspicion strikes again, making me look like a jerk. "Sorry," Bethany said. "I'll shut up now."

"Stellar idea," Aaron said dryly.

"Do you know why Marigold would have your social security card?" Charley asked. "Did you give that to her, too?"

Probably stole it—took it from her own cousin. Maybe Olive was right, and Marigold was just a thief. And maybe she took something that made someone angry enough to kill her—something like fifty thousand dollars.

Jen shook her head. "It must have gotten mixed up when we switched purses."

"Ah." Charley nodded. "Makes sense. Well, have a safe trip. The department will be in touch as the case develops."

"Fine." Aaron steered Jen back toward the ticket booth, but before they could get more than a step or two, Olive scurried out of the Honor Roll and blocked their way.

"Oh, you poor dears! I just wanted to tell you again how very sorry I am for everything that happened. I know it's a lot to ask, but it'd mean so much to me if you'd stay in Newbridge a few more days."

Aaron sneered. "Why would we want to spend any more time here?"

"I'm organizing a memorial for Marigold on Saturday afternoon here at the station. I think it'll be healing for the whole community. We'll have some yummy food and then a nice little service where people can talk about their memories of Marigold. The good ones, obviously."

"It's not a bad idea, actually," Charley said. "We should have the final police report filed by then, so you can at least go home with a complete picture of what happened to your cousin. Some closure."

"Well," Jen began, "you see, we—"

"We can't really afford two or three more nights in a quaint little B&B now that we have a funeral to pay for," Aaron cut in, acid in his voice.

"Right." Jen nodded, her eyes sad.

Olive shook her head and clucked sympathetically. "No, no, that won't do. You should come stay with me and Garrett. We have a spare room in the cottage now that the kids have all flown the coop. I'll even make you my special waffles for breakfast. I won't let you say no!"

Jen and Aaron looked at each other for a long moment.

"It's a great idea," Charley said. "And bonus, once the final report is filed, we'll probably be able to release Marigold's assets to you, too."

"You mean the check?" Aaron asked.

Charley nodded. "She didn't have a will, so anything that was hers will go to Jen as her next of kin."

"That'd help you pay for the funeral," Olive said. "Please say you'll stay! It's only until Saturday, though of course you can stay longer if you want."

Jen nodded. "I can't thank you enough."

"Don't mention it!" Olive chirped, and bustled them off just as the 10:55 train pulled into the station.

"Want some stew?" Bethany asked Charley as soon as they were gone.

Charley wrinkled her nose. "Nah. Oysters are not really my thing."

Chapter 6

The spicy oyster stew was not the runaway success that Bethany had hoped. For one, ridership on the 10:55 was down—way down—from yesterday, and the 11:55 was only marginally better. Apparently a person getting squashed on the tracks put a real damper on the commuter train business. And secondly, it seemed like fifty percent of customers were like Milo and didn't like spicy food, and the other fifty percent were like Charley and didn't like oysters.

Maybe it was a good thing Milo hadn't tried the stew. After all, no food feature was better than a negative one. She could see the headline now: "Souperb Soups: Spotlight on Failure." She sighed. So much for the one-hour workday. She put her elbow on the counter and rested her chin on her hand while she waited for the 12:55 train.

Trevor walked by, whistling, and stopped when he saw her glum expression. "Bad day?"

"You win some, you lose some. Want some oyster stew? On the house."

"Can't. Maintenance rounds. Gotta check the ol' checklist. I'm just looking for Caboose—he likes to go through the tunnels with me." He jangled his ring of keys. "Usually this sound makes him come running."

"Hey, you got your keys back. Is that what you were looking for yesterday?"

"Yeah," he said sheepishly, turning faintly pink. "I was hoping I had an extra set stashed somewhere, but I didn't. Then I

found them when I was taking out the trash last night! Someone threw them away."

"You think Marigold tossed them before she went to meet
the train?"

Trevor shrugged. "Doesn't matter now."

"You're not even a little curious? I mean, it's not like she
planned to be killed, so why would she throw them away? If
she'd had a regular, non-murdered day, you would have come
looking for the keys and chewed her out. It had to be the killer
who tossed them!"

Trevor looked skeptical. "Maybe it was just someone who
found them on the floor."

"If I found a big fat ring of keys, I'd turn them in to the stationmaster."

"Well, you're not everyone, and not everyone wants to deal
with Ben." Trevor scanned the concourse and shook his key
ring, still on the lookout for Caboose.

Wait. The cat had been by the restrooms when Marigold
was killed! If Trevor was doing his rounds at that time, why was
Caboose prowling around the hallway by the restrooms instead
of in the maintenance tunnels? Bethany stood up straight, a
burning question propelling her upright. "If you didn't have
your keys until you took the garbage out at night, how did you
do your maintenance rounds yesterday? Did you borrow Ben's
keys?"

Trevor took a few steps toward the kiosk and leaned in,
looking faintly ill. In a low voice he said, "Can you keep a secret? I feel terrible—I didn't actually do my rounds yesterday.
I hid in the maintenance closet so that Ben wouldn't realize I
didn't have my keys. He was already so angry that I'd loaned my

keys to Marigold that I was afraid of telling him that she hadn't returned them. I thought he might fire me, and this would definitely be terrible timing to lose my job. Did you know my wife was due *yesterday*?"

"I didn't know that. So wait, you were lying about being in the tunnels when Marigold was killed?"

"I only nudged the truth a little bit sideways. I was in the maintenance closet instead of the tunnels. Either way, I couldn't see anything—I wasn't on the platform. I wish I had been, though. Maybe I could have stopped it from happening if I had done my rounds."

"You realize that means she might have been with someone on the platform." Bethany shook her head.

"She should have given my keys back to me! Then she wouldn't be dead, and I wouldn't be *this close* to losing my job!" Trevor pinched his fingers together to show exactly how close he meant. "She's so selfish! She knew we needed the money."

Bethany's ears perked up. *Did Trevor know about the check?* "The money?"

"Yeah, my paycheck. I told her Ben would can me if I didn't do my rounds. She knew about the new baby and everything. And she still didn't return the keys. What a piece of work, making me look bad in front of my boss. But I guess the joke was on her in the end."

Not a very funny joke. Trevor didn't seem to care very much that Marigold had been murdered. He cared a whole lot more about keeping his job. Was he willing to kill to keep it, though? It was hard to tell if he was being serious, but he definitely needed the money.

"Did you know that Marigold had fifty thousand dollars on her when she was killed? In her bra. Murderer took her purse, but didn't know about the check. Or at least, didn't know where it was."

Trevor's jaw dropped. "If I'd known she had that much cash, I'd have asked her for a loan!"

His surprise seemed genuine enough. "Any idea where she got it?" Bethany asked.

"Nah. Well, maybe she took it from Ben's office when she went in there to get her bag."

She laughed out loud, thinking of Ben with his adding machine. "Since when does Ben have fifty thousand dollars?"

"Since, uh"—Trevor scratched his head—"Monday afternoon? He got an anonymous donation to the restoration fund in that exact amount. He told us about it at poker that night."

"What?!"

"I know, can you believe that? Someone just giving fifty thou away. Some people are too rich for their own good." He jangled his keys again, and Caboose came running from the Honor Roll. Trevor glanced at the clock. "About time, you darn cat. Shoot, I have to hustle now to finish up on time. Good luck unloading that oyster stew."

Bethany settled her chin back on her hand while she contemplated something uncomfortable—she shared Trevor's suspicions that Marigold had stolen the check. That wasn't so uncomfortable, even though she didn't usually see eye-to-eye with the bumbling custodian. What was making her stomach hurt was that it meant Ben had a real motive to kill Marigold. Bethany realized that for all her nosiness, she didn't really want to find out the identity of the murderer—not if it was someone she knew.

The 12:55 train came in before she had time to think much about it, and she served a steady stream of customers. By the time the crowd of passengers thinned out, she was pretty much down to the bottom of her pot. Sales were not as disappointing as she thought they'd be; she just had to work a couple of hours longer.

She erased the chalk board and served herself the last bowl. Even after a few hours on the warmer, the stew was still delicious—fragrant and piquant. *Hmm, a food feature wouldn't have been the end of the world, even if the soup wasn't for everyone.*

As she ate the last few bites, she noticed Ryan walk through the entrance to Newbridge Station, a watch cap pulled down over his forehead and the collar of his Army surplus jacket turned up. Her first instinct was to duck behind the counter to avoid having another exhausting conversation with him about her soup artistry, but with her luck, he'd probably see her.

"Ryan!" she called to him as he walked toward the Honor Roll. He startled and looked up. When he recognized her, he raised a hand in greeting. He stopped for a moment, apparently torn about whether to come over to the kiosk or pick up the leftover bread from Olive. She waved at him. "Stay warm out there!"

He nodded and flashed a brilliant smile before opening the door to the bakery and going inside. She sighed with relief and hurried to close the curtains around her kiosk and hang up the "closed" sign before he came back out.

While Bethany cleaned up the kiosk, she reflected on the million dollar question about Marigold's murder. Well, actually, the fifty-thousand-dollar question. Now that she had a minute to gather her thoughts, she reasoned that maybe the dollar amounts were a coincidence. Just because Marigold had fifty K and the donation was fifty K didn't mean they were the same money. The anonymous donation was probably safe and sound in the historic restoration fund.

After all, Marigold had been *not* selling smoothies for months now. She had to have some other source of money to pay her bills. Maybe the check in her bra was just a simple errand—she could have withdrawn her funds to move them to a new account at another bank. Or maybe she was putting a down payment on a house or buying a food truck. There were a million explanations, and it was silly to jump to the conclusion that Marigold had stolen the money from Ben's office.

Still...it didn't hurt to ask if the restoration fund donation was missing, did it?

* * * *

BEN WAS LAYING ON THE floor under his desk with one arm flung over his face when Bethany entered the stationmaster's office. With his other arm, he motioned for her to close the door. "Please tell me you have some good news. Anything. Tell me it's not going to rain tomorrow."

Bethany checked the weather app on her phone. "Sixty percent chance of rain."

Ben groaned. "You're terrible at this good news thing."

"Are you lying on the floor because you're upset about the restoration fund donation being stolen?"

Ben sat up so fast that he banged his head on the underside of his desk. "How did you know about that?"

"I didn't know for sure, but the cops said Marigold had a big check stuffed in her bra, and Trevor said you got a big anonymous donation to the fund. Plus, I knew that Marigold had the keys to your office yesterday. Well, the keys to everything." She kneeled down beside Ben. "Do you want some ice for that?"

He rubbed his forehead and stood up, wobbling only slightly. "No, I'm fine. I mean, I've been better, but I don't need first aid."

Bethany got to her feet and brushed the carpet lint off the knees of her black jeans. "I guess she took the check when she came in here to get her purse."

"Evidently. Trevor really screwed the pooch by lending her his keys. He's not supposed to let *anyone* touch them. I'd like to fire the guy, but it'd take weeks to get a new custodian up to speed."

"He thought he was helping you out by doing your girl-friend a favor."

Ben picked up his desk chair and slammed it down on the floor. "She wasn't my girlfriend!"

Bethany put up her hands defensively and took a step back.

Ben shook his head. "Sorry. People just keep saying that, and it isn't true."

"If she wasn't your girlfriend, then why didn't you go to the police when you realized she stole the check?" Bethany eyed the door and mentally planned her escape route, just in case Ben's temper flared again. He didn't blow up, though. Instead, he hung his head.

"Well, I told her about the money at our poker night. She wouldn't have even known about it if I hadn't said anything."

Bethany snorted. "That doesn't mean she had a right to take it. I mean, Trevor heard about the donation, and he didn't steal it. And if he had, you'd have reported him!"

"I probably would have if it were Trevor," Ben admitted. "Or Garrett—he was playing that night, too. But there were some complications when it came to Marigold. The morning after the poker game, she told me that if I didn't give her the donation money, she'd report me to the ZamRail regional director for a hostile workplace. Harassment."

Bethany gasped. "But why? She didn't have any evidence of that, did she?"

Ben sank heavily into his desk chair and put his head in his hands. "Actually, she did. She has all kinds of text messages and love letters from me."

"Well, I'm sure you have the same from her, right? What's the big deal if you had an off-hours flirtation?"

"That's the thing. Once I looked at the messages, I realized that her replies were always neutral and professional on paper, even though she told me she loved me in person. That's why I said..." he broke off as his voice choked.

"That she wasn't your girlfriend," Bethany finished. "You thought she was, but when she tried to blackmail you for the donation money, you realized she was just pretending. And you gave her the check because you didn't want to lose your career, which is why you didn't report it as a theft to the police."

He jerked his head up from his hands. "No! That's just it! I thought about it all day Tuesday and decided that restoring the station was more important than my pension. So when she came by Tuesday night to collect the check, I told her no way. I wasn't going to do it. She screamed at me, but I stayed firm. I guess that's when she decided to steal it."

Bethany nodded. "And she left her purse in your office on purpose so she had an excuse to come back, preferably when you weren't there."

"That idiot Trevor let her in," Ben said bitterly. "I realized the check was gone as soon as I got to work on Wednesday. I confronted her about it and told her that she had twelve hours to return the money, or I'd call the cops. I said my career wasn't important to me if it meant Newbridge Station crumbled to the ground. Surprisingly, she apologized and agreed to bring it back."

"Or said she would, anyway," Bethany said dryly. She'd already lost faith that Marigold had any good intentions.

"I think she meant it. I believed her, anyway." Ben shrugged.

"So what'd you do after she promised to return the money?"

"I reprimanded Trevor for loaning out his keys."

Bethany nodded. That matched up with Trevor's version of events, too. "Right, I saw you when I came into the station. Then what?"

"Back to my office to do the bookkeeping."

"And after that?"

Ben stared at her, puzzled. "I went to the men's room. While I was in there, I got the emergency call from the 10:55 train that someone had been hit."

"Hmm." Bethany frowned. The last time she'd asked Ben about his alibi, he'd said he was in his office when he got the call.

"What?"

"Well. Your story changed a little bit. You didn't mention the restroom visit before."

"I just remembered. After I ran some numbers, I went to the bathroom."

"OK." Bethany's heart sank. She knew for a fact that he wasn't in the men's room at the time of the murder because *Jen* was in the men's room. She'd seen Jen go in with her own eyes. Why was Ben lying about this? It's not like being in the restroom was a better alibi than being in his office. Either way, nobody could corroborate it.

What was Ben hiding behind his wishy-washy non-alibi? Could it be murder? Maybe he gave Marigold the money and then changed his mind and asked for it back. He might have killed her when she wouldn't hand over the check.

"I wish I'd done the rounds that day. I always wait on the platform until the train pulls in." Ben shook his head. "If someone was trying to hurt her, I'd have stuck up for her."

Bethany shook her head in disbelief that anyone could be that forgiving. "Really? You don't think Marigold might have deserved it after what she did to you? I mean, if she stole fifty grand from you and you weren't mad enough to push her off a platform, imagine what she must have done to someone else!"

Ben shook his head. "She didn't steal from me. She stole from the fund, or from the donor if you want to get specific. I know what you're getting at, but I didn't hurt Marigold."

Oops, and I thought I was being subtle. Bethany crossed her arms, her face burning. "Well, who do you think killed her, then? Any theories?"

"I don't want to cast blame."

"But...?"

Ben winced. "Well, Trevor asked me if he could borrow some money last week. He had some debts—gambling debts—that he wanted to pay back before the baby came. I know he owed Marigold at least a grand. Possibly she called in the debt? That might have led to a fight on the platform when he was doing his rounds. I'm sure he didn't mean to do it."

Except he didn't do the rounds, Bethany said silently. *Trevor wasn't there.* Or he said he wasn't there. Now that she thought about it, neither Trevor nor Ben had a real alibi. She had to sort out which parts of their stories made sense and which didn't—she couldn't keep taking them at their word, especially when those words changed every time she talked to them!

"That's a decent theory," she said. "But if he needed money, why didn't he steal the big fat check?"

"Well, her purse was missing, right? He probably thought the check was in there." Ben shook his head. "I still can't believe she's gone. I thought I'd get to yell at her again, and maybe even reconcile."

Bethany softened at his words. "You loved her in spite of her bad behavior."

Ben nodded. "Shameful, isn't it? What we do for people. What we can forgive."

• • • •

KIMMY CROSSED HER ARMS as she stood in the middle of their little yellow kitchen. "Well, *I* can't forgive her for stealing the restoration fund money. Who did she think would suffer if the station closed? You, Olive, everyone who works in that place, not to mention all the people in Newbridge who use the train. She's the definition of selfishness."

Charley swiped a pinch of cheese from the cutting board where Bethany was grating parmesan for their pasta. "Shouldn't speak ill of the dead," she mumbled through her mouthful.

Kimmy stuck out her tongue. "Isn't that what you do all day? Go around uncovering the dirty secrets, the ulterior motives, the ugly impulses?"

Charley grabbed her chest and pretended to fall on the floor. "That one hurt, Kimmy. You got me right in the heart."

"Well, isn't it? You dig up the stuff nobody is supposed to know. It's like people have been reading a book of their lives, and you show up to read them a new chapter that changes the context of everything they've experienced. You tell them, 'No, this person you thought was your loving partner or child is actually a bad guy.' And then you ask them why."

Charley's forehead creased. "Geez, Kimmy, what crawled up your butt? What I do every day is go out there to make sure the bad guys are caught so they don't hurt people. That's it."

"Who are you going to interrogate now?" Kimmy pursed her lips. "Which of our friends?"

"Cut it out, please," Bethany said from the sink, where she was draining the pasta. "You two are driving me crazy with all your bickering."

Charley ignored her, eyes trained on Kimmy. "Is that why you're picking this fight? You think I'm going to arrest someone you know and like for the murder of someone you didn't like?"

Kimmy's chin quivered, and she sat down hard on the stool by the counter. "Yeah, pretty much."

"Aw." Charley crossed the kitchen and pulled Kimmy to her chest. She kissed the top of her head and left her lips there an extra moment. "You know I have to be fair. I have to do my job according to the law, not according to Kimmy, as much as I'd like to."

"Do you think you have enough evidence for an arrest?" Bethany asked quietly. She dished the hot pasta onto three plates and smothered the noodles with puttanesca.

Charley sprinkled some of the parmesan on her plate of food and sat down at the counter. She stuck her fork into the pasta and twirled it around, but stopped before taking a bite. "Yeah. From what you've said, there's a lot of evidence pointing to one person."

Kimmy put her hands over her ears. "Na na na na, I can't hear you!"

"Ben?" Bethany asked, putting a plate on the counter in front of Kimmy. Charley nodded. "But what about Trevor? Or Olive? Or Jen—maybe she got tired of being pushed around! Or Aaron—that guy didn't want to stay a minute longer than he had to."

Charley put down her fork. "Ben lost fifty thousand dollars, his relationship, and potentially his job because of Marigold. He had the strongest motive to kill her, by far, and he has no alibi. I know he's not evil, Kimmy. He probably didn't mean to hurt her—things just got heated. He pushed her, and she fell. It's terrible and wrong, but it's not evil."

Kimmy dropped her hands from her ears and stared dolefully at her pasta. Charley put her arm around Kimmy's shoulders and squeezed, murmuring sympathetically in her ear.

Bethany turned away and studiously ate her dinner, embarrassed to watch their intimate moment. It'd been a long time since anyone comforted her like that. She'd been so focused on getting Souperb Soups up and running that she'd completely neglected dating and most of her friendships for the better part of a year, and to be honest, she missed those connections. Maybe it was time to do something about that now that a couple of prospects were on the radar.

Not that Ryan is a prospect. He was just cute, not dating material, even if he had the brightest smile on the eastern seaboard. She should definitely set her sights on someone more like Milo, who clearly cared about his career and had a more normal life.

"I have to go to the station," Charley said abruptly. She pushed back her stool and rinsed her empty plate in the sink.

"Right now?" Kimmy asked. "It's almost midnight. Can't you wait until the morning?"

Charley shook her head. "I need to update my report with the new information Bethany told me about the restoration fund theft and Ben's changing alibi. We'll question him about it in the morning, most likely—I don't think we'll be breaking down any doors tonight."

"But you'll probably arrest him," Bethany said, guilt souring her stomach.

Charley nodded and seemed to recognize what Bethany was feeling. "You did the right thing, telling me."

"What if I'm wrong? What if it was someone else? You know I'm too suspicious sometimes." Bethany anxiously tapped her fork against her plate, the *ting ting ting* matching the pounding in her ears.

"Don't worry—if Ben didn't push Marigold, we'll find out. I'm not interested in arresting innocent people."

"Then why can't you wait a couple of days, so we—*you* have a chance to ask more questions? Rule out the other possibilities first?"

Kimmy nodded. "Marigold's memorial is on Saturday, and Olive has put so much energy into planning it. If Ben is arrested, it'll ruin it for her. Can't you just give her two more days? It's not even two whole days...you could arrest him after the memorial on Saturday afternoon."

"And by then I'll—I mean, *you'll* be really really sure," Bethany added hopefully.

Charley rubbed her face with both hands. "This is crazy. I'm going to arrest a murderer, and I feel like I'm letting you both down. As much as I love you, Kimmy, I have to do this by the book. I'm sorry. I understand if you don't want me to come back." She grabbed her coat and left.

Kimmy stared at the closed door, her mouth half-open. Bethany felt terrible for her. If she'd just kept her suspicions about Ben to herself for a little bit longer, Charley wouldn't have had to make such a painful choice. "I'm sorry—I feel like this is my fault."

Kimmy shook her head. "Did you hear that?"

"I know. She's not coming back."

"Not that—she said she loves me!" Kimmy turned to her with huge, glowing eyes. One look at her friend's expression, and Bethany couldn't help grinning.

"I did hear that. Loud and clear."

Chapter 7

heerful. That was the goal for Friday's soup of the day. Something to help people forget the ugliness of the week. *Curry lentil, maybe?* No, she'd learned her lesson with the spicy oyster stew. A curry might be warm and uplifting, but it was too challenging for some Newbridge residents. Today required something that evoked a feel-good happiness that was both innocent and nostalgic. *Classic tomato.* Yes!

Invigorated by the decision, Bethany pedaled faster along the Newbridge waterfront, whizzing past the commercial docks where she often bought fresh seafood, the park with the curved sandy beach, and the houseboats and small sailing craft in the marina.

Prep at Café Sabine was simple. She had leftover chicken stock from earlier in the week in the freezer, the tomatoes were from a can (sweeter and riper than fresh ones, this time of year), and she had plenty of onions and garlic stashed in the back of Kimmy's pantry. Yet, even after the soup had burbled on the back burner of the café's enormous range for forty minutes and was seasoned perfectly, it was still missing something.

"Basil?" Bethany asked, holding a spoon out to Kimmy. "Thyme?"

Kimmy tasted the soup, smacking her lips, and tossed the spoon into the sink. "Cream."

Bethany giggled. "You always say cream."

"And I'm usually right." Kimmy stirred her own soup of the day, a delicate vichyssoise.

"I wish Charley were here to give an opinion, too," Bethany said, tasting the soup herself. It was fine, but maybe just a bit under-salted. Kimmy was right, cream wouldn't hurt, either.

"She'd just say it needed chili peppers."

Bethany nodded and gave a halfhearted smile. "She's usually here by now. I guess she's probably busy at the train station."

"Probably," Kimmy said, her voice tight.

"I'm kind of afraid to go over there. I don't really want to see Ben if I can help it, to be honest."

Kimmy turned to face Bethany with tears in her eyes. "Don't feel bad. You didn't betray him, Bethany. He's the one who did something wrong. He betrayed all of us."

"I know, but I wish I felt more sure about it."

"Hopefully he'll just confess once he realizes the police know it's him and save everyone some grief."

Bethany nodded. "Except Olive—she's still going to be bummed that her memorial service won't be perfect."

"We'll just have to make sure it's better than perfect. Plus, how great will it be for Jen to go home knowing that the person who killed her cousin is behind bars? That would have to be comforting."

"You're starting to sound like Charley." Bethany winked.

Kimmy blushed. "Not really, but I *am* starting to appreciate that Charley is so by the book. It's hard enough dating a cop, but imagine dating a cop that you didn't think was following the rules. I mean, if she'll bend the rules for her friends, that's pretty much the end, isn't it? That's corruption, even if it's benign. Another time it might not be."

Bethany nodded. "Very true. And with Charley's ambition, she'll probably be police chief someday. Who better than someone who is so ethical that she won't even delay filing a report long enough to have dessert? On that note, I should play by the rules and get to work, even though I dread seeing Ben. He'll know I'm the one who told."

"Maybe they arrested him already, and you won't have to talk to him."

"Ugh, I'm not going to hope for that, either. I'm going to hope that he had some magical proof that he didn't do it, and they moved on to another suspect. I hope he's sitting in his office, angry at me for causing trouble. That's what I hope." Bethany gave a firm nod.

Kimmy looked at her with sad eyes. "You do realize that if Ben is cleared, that means someone else did it. Who else would you prefer go to jail? Trevor, when his wife is about to pop?"

"I'd prefer it was nobody! I hope it was someone none of us have ever seen or heard of before."

"Then the killer probably will get away with it, and might even kill someone else. Is that what you're hoping for?"

"Ugh." Bethany brandished a spoon like a gun. "Who are you, and what have you done with my Kimmy?"

Kimmy sighed. "I'm just trying to make a point."

"Point taken. I'll stop hoping and just make my tomato soup like a good girl until the nice men figure it out." Bethany flashed a sickly-sweet smile.

"And Charley. The nice men and Charley. She's our only hope."

• • • •

AS SOON AS BETHANY set foot inside Newbridge Station, she heard the shouts echoing down the concourse. Olive was standing out in front of the Honor Roll, watching, and so was everyone else in the station. Two police officers were hand-cuffing Ben near the ticket booth while Charley read him his rights. Ben struggled, his loafers slipping on the worn marble tiles as he fought to avoid being cuffed, but he had little hope against the two strong officers.

Olive had a hand over her mouth, her brows furrowed with concern. "Oh, I hope they don't hurt him. I really do."

Bethany's throat ached with unshed tears. A cycle of blame spiraled like a cyclone in her mind. This is my fault for telling on Ben. This is Ben's fault for killing Marigold. This is Marigold's fault for stealing the money.

Olive couldn't take her eyes off the scene. "They didn't have to do it like this—so publicly. They could have done it in his office." Bethany was so overwhelmed with emotion, she couldn't even respond. The officers finally got the cuffs on Ben and escorted him to the door. As he passed them, he spotted Bethany.

"I didn't do this, Bethany! You know I didn't! Find out who's to blame. You find out!" His eyes bored into her even as the door closed, and she could no longer hear him through the glass. She could read his lips, though—*you find out, you find out, you find out*—as they put him into the back of a squad car.

"What a shame." Olive fluttered her hand. "What a waste of a nice man like Ben Kovac."

"Even nice men do bad things sometimes. I'm surprised, though, I guess. I thought it was *possible* he did it, but I guess deep down I didn't believe he was capable. I somehow thought that Charley would clear him today."

"Desperate people do stupid things, I'm sorry to say," Olive murmured. "They're wrapped up in their own little world, not thinking about consequences."

Bethany nodded sadly. "Help me lift the soup onto the warmer?"

"Sure." Olive trailed behind her over to the kiosk, and they lifted the heavy stock pot together. "Bigger vat than usual, eh?"

"I'm trying a new stock pot. I sell out so quickly that I figured I'd better increase capacity so the 12:55 folks aren't always shortchanged." Bethany wrote "Nostalgic Tomato" on the chalk board. "What do you think about pairing this with grilled cheese sandwiches on your classic white bread?"

"Or cheesy biscuits?" Olive suggested. "I don't have a grill."

"That'd work. Or you could make grilled cheese in the oven—have you tried that?"

Olive clapped her hands gleefully. "No, but what a fantastic idea. That way I can make a bunch at once, too. I'm going to go do a test batch to make sure it works before the rush. That reminds me, I wanted to ask you if you'd make a special soup for Marigold's memorial on Saturday. I know you don't usually cook on the weekends, but it's for a good cause. I can't pay you much, but—"

"Of course I will, and don't say another word about money. Is there anything else I can help with? Especially now that Ben can't be here?" Bethany hated to remind Olive about Ben's arrest, but she also wanted to keep her promise to Kimmy to help make Olive's event better than perfect, and that meant planning ahead.

"You know? Life goes on," Olive said, her mouth straight and set in a very un-Olive-like expression. "We can't make everything right, now can we?"

"No, I guess not. We just have to do our best for Marigold's family. How are your houseguests? Hanging in there?"

Olive nodded, her face brightening. "They're anxious to get home, of course, but they seem relieved that the killer has been caught." She nodded over to the bakery, where Jen and Aaron sat in a table at the window. They looked more glum than relieved, staring at the cups of coffee on the table in front of them. Jen kept wiping her nose on the sleeve of her jacket until Aaron handed her a napkin. For such a prickly guy, he was so tender and gentlemanly with Jen. It reminded Bethany a little of Kimmy and Charley.

"Why don't I come with you while you test-bake the cheese sandwiches, and I can talk with Jen about what soup she thinks would be best for the memorial?"

Olive nodded, and Bethany followed her into the Honor Roll. A wave of warm, pastry-scented air enveloped her the moment she stepped through the swinging glass door. Bethany's stomach rumbled audibly, and Olive chuckled.

"Common reaction. Care for a multiplication muffin?"

Bethany nodded eagerly, and Olive brought her a citrus-scented muffin with an "X" made of orange zest on top. She thanked Olive and took the plate over to the table where Jen and Aaron sat. "Mind if I join you two?"

Jen shook her head and moved Marigold's purse off the table so there was room for Bethany's plate. Bethany sat and, to combat the awkward silence that followed, crammed a big piece of the muffin in her mouth. She chewed while they stared at her. "Um. How are you doing?"

"How do you think?" Aaron snorted. "What do you want?"

Bethany swallowed. *Tough crowd.* "Well, I'm planning to cook for Marigold's memorial, and I wanted to ask about her favorites. What do you think she'd have liked?"

Aaron rolled his eyes. "If you want to know what she liked, you should probably ask someone else."

"Stop," Jen said. "It's not important now."

Bethany tried to suppress her curiosity out of respect for Jen's grief, but it bubbled to the surface anyway. "What do you mean? Who knows her better than you?"

"You must have noticed that she had a habit of 'borrowing'"—he made air quotes around the word with his fingers—"things she liked. I doubt she had any thoughts of her own."

"I noticed, but I thought it was just me she was copying."

"Not just you," Aaron said.

"Interesting. So why do you think she 'borrowed' the money from Ben's office? I mean, he'd obviously know right away that she did it, so how did she think she'd get away with it?"

"How did she think she'd get away with stealing your business concept?" Jen murmured. "She just gets what she wants."

"And that's why she's dead." Aaron sounded so satisfied that Bethany would have thought he was the murderer, if he hadn't been on the train that hit her.

Wait. Was he on the train? Of course, he and Jen said he was, but what if he wasn't? What if he was on the platform *not* because he'd exited the train, but because he had just pushed Marigold onto the tracks? Bethany's heart raced.

She forced a smile onto her face. "You must be relieved that her killer has been caught."

Jen shook her head. "I just want to go home. This whole trip has been a fiasco from start to finish. I don't know why I thought it was a good idea."

The right thing to do would be to leave Jen and Aaron alone, when they clearly didn't want to talk to her. But Ben's words kept echoing in her mind. *You find out, you find out.* If there was even a chance that Aaron wasn't on that train, or that Ben was telling the truth about being in the restroom when Marigold was killed, Bethany had to find out. "I'm sorry to have bothered you. I know this is a hard time. Just out of curiosity, though...did you see Ben when you came out of the restroom on Wednesday morning?"

They both stared at her wordlessly. She kept talking to fill the awkward silence. "You know, he said he went to the restroom at the time of the murder, but before that he said he was in his office, so I wondered if you saw him. I mean, I saw you go in the men's room, but he can't have gone to the men's room if you were in there, but maybe he went in as you were coming out? Is that possible? Did you see him?"

"No," Jen said flatly, and Aaron scraped back his chair and stood up.

"Enough of this. You need to leave now. She doesn't want to talk about it any more. Come on Jen, let's go."

Bethany bit her lip. Ugh, she had to ask. "Where are you going?"

Jen closed her eyes. In a tired voice, she said, "Probably just walking down to the marina and back. We could use some air."

"Enjoy. Um, there's a little tea-and-toast shop on Sixth Street, down by the park, in case you get cold."

Aaron nodded curtly and held the bakery door open for Jen on their way out. As Bethany watched them through the bakery windows, Olive came up beside her with a cheese sandwich on a small plate.

"Try this."

Bethany took a bite. *Crunchy, creamy, salty, buttery*—everything a grilled cheese sandwich should be. "It's genius."

"Why, thank you." Olive curtsied. "You better get over to your booth. Looks like you have a line already."

Bethany did a little internal happy dance. *Nostalgic Tomato for the win.* Yesterday's slowdown was just a fluke, a blip. And to her pleasant surprise, Milo was first in line.

"Hey, stranger." She grinned at him. She wondered if he was here for the food or the company. "Is that your crime hat or your soup hat?"

"Definitely the soup hat. Where have you been?"

Maybe he was here for both. She tied on her apron and filled a container with the rich tomato-y goodness. "I was over at the Honor Roll talking to Marigold's cousin and her fiancé about the memorial service tomorrow. They're pretty upset about everything, understandably."

Milo whipped his head around toward the bakery. "They're here? Where?"

She pointed toward the exit. "See the woman in the red coat? That's Jen. They're just leaving now. Said they were going on a walk down to the marina."

Milo put both hands on the kiosk counter, an apologetic grimace on his face. "Listen, I—"

"Buddy, hurry up. I gotta catch a train!" the burly construction worker behind him said.

"I've gotta run. Doing a profile on Marigold for the paper, and I desperately need to talk to her family. Sorry?" He dashed off.

Bethany rolled her eyes. *Of course.* She slid the container of soup to the construction worker and put the three bucks he handed her in the till. "The Honor Roll has grilled cheese sandwiches to go with," she said automatically, watching Milo's back disappear out the front doors of the station. *Figures.*

Chapter 8

Friday afternoon

As the lunch rush ended, and the bottom of her stock pot was in sight, Bethany noticed Trevor walking by without his usual confident swagger. Instead of his coveralls, he wore a too-small suit jacket and a stationmaster's cap that he kept taking on and off and twisting in his hands. Caboose tagged along at his heels.

"Want some lunch before I close up?" she asked. He glanced up at her chalk board and then nodded. "Don't worry, it's a safe bet. Nothing weird in it."

His face relaxed, and he broke into a grin. "Phew! Last time I tried your soup, it had tails in it!"

Bethany chuckled. "That must have been the gumbo. The tail-on shrimp supposedly make it taste better, but I got enough complaints that I'll probably take those tails off next time."

Trevor dug into the soup there at the counter, dripping some onto his jacket. She handed him a napkin, and he scrubbed furiously at his lapel and muttered to himself. "Can't do anything right...stupid monkey suit."

"You seem a little stressed out. Is it about taking on the stationmaster role?"

He nodded. "That, and Julie is in labor, but I can't leave the station until the last evening train. She'll probably have the baby by then, and I will never live that down." His phone pinged in his pocket, and he fumbled as he pulled it out, his hands shaking as he checked the message. "See? She's already mad at me, and it's only noon. No way that baby is staying inside for another seven or eight hours!"

"There has to be someone to take over for you. Can't you call ZamRail to send a substitute from another station?"

"I did. They said no one is available until Monday, and if I want to keep my job, I need to fill in today. It's just the safety stuff, but even that is a lot."

Bethany nodded sympathetically. "I guess you can't do both jobs indefinitely. They'll have to hire someone quickly."

"Yeah, the ZamRail person I talked to this morning said the station might have to close until they find a new station-master. They'll just bus the commuters to Oldbridge until then. It could take them a month to find someone new!"

"Bad news for Souperb and the Honor Roll—it's not like we can serve food at Oldbridge." She sighed. "We'll have to close."

"Bad news for Caboose, too. I don't know who'll take him while the station's under construction. And it won't be easy to find a replacement for Ben," Trevor said glumly. "I know I complained about the guy a lot, but he's one of the best stationmasters around. He does the work of two or three people. Don't get me wrong, he's kind of a jerk, and if he killed someone he should be in jail, but I don't know...it's like when your dad's a jerk. You still love the guy."

Bethany nodded. "Do you think he did it?"

"I'm not sure." Trevor scooped up Caboose and cradled him, scratching behind the cat's ears until he purred with pleasure. Seeing him hold Caboose so gently made Bethany realize what a great dad he was going to be.

"The cops are pretty sure. And I know he lied to me about his alibi. First he said he was in his office, and then he said he was in the restroom. He claimed he forgot, but do you forgot something so important like where you were when you got the call that someone was hit by a train?"

"Huh," Trevor said, his face and shoulders relaxing as he stroked the cat's belly. "I actually saw him coming out of the men's room at 11:00. I was peeking out the door of the maintenance closet."

"You know the exact time?"

"Yeah, I do. My rounds end around that time, so I was checking to make sure Ben didn't see me leaving the closet—then he'd know I didn't do my rounds. And it's a good thing I did, because I would have run right into him."

Bethany gasped. "But this means that Ben was telling the truth—his alibi stands up! Jen must have left the restroom just before him, or not noticed him in the hall because she was in a hurry to get back to the kiosk. *Oh no*—poor Ben! We have to call Charley and tell her she has the wrong guy! He couldn't have done it."

"Slow your roll," Trevor said thoughtfully. He set Caboose gently on the floor, and the cat flopped down on his feet like a wet towel. "It actually explains how he *could* have done it. He could have used his keys to access the maintenance tunnel in the men's room, gone down to the platform, pushed Marigold in front of the train, and then come back without anyone seeing him."

"Wait, there's a tunnel entrance in the bathroom?!"

Trevor nodded. "We keep it locked. But Ben has keys, of course."

Bethany's heart sank. That explained how Ben got to the platform and back without anyone seeing him on the concourse. And it made perfect sense why he said he'd been in his office the first time she asked, but then changed his answer to the restroom, on the off chance that someone saw him exiting it at that time. It was closer to the truth, too—he *had* gotten the call about someone on the tracks while he was in the restroom, after he'd fled the scene of the crime.

The timeline seemed tight, but it was possible if Ben and Marigold didn't argue too long before he pushed her. But... "Wouldn't Ben have been worried that he'd see you in the tunnels? If you were doing your rounds, you should have been right there when he was on the platform. He'd have known that."

Trevor opened his mouth, started to say something, and then stopped.

"Did you notice him carrying anything when he was leaving the restroom?"

"Like a weapon? No, not that I remember." Trevor shook his head vigorously.

"Not like a weapon," Bethany said. "Like a purse. A black, patent-leather, vintage Chanel purse."

Bethany thought she saw Trevor's eyes widen, just for a moment. "Nope." He looked over his shoulder at the station clock. "We better get going on the rounds before the 12:55 comes in. The station never sleeps. Thanks for the soup." He patted the counter and walked away quickly, shoes squeaking on the marble floors as Caboose scampered behind him.

Bethany took a deep breath. It was important not to jump to conclusions. She knew the murderer took a black purse from

Marigold—she'd just been to the bank, so of course she had her purse with her. If Ben was the killer, he must have hidden the purse somewhere before he left the restroom. The tunnels, maybe? But if Ben wasn't the killer, then the killer would have the purse—or know where it was.

Bethany dialed Charley's number as she watched Trevor move toward the other side of the concourse. Was he going to the stationmaster's office—or was he going to find the purse? "Charley? Where are you?"

"With Kimmy. She made those cookies again."

"Can you come across the street—like, now? It's kind of urgent."

"On my way."

Charley skidded through the door, madeleines in hand, all of thirty seconds later. "What is it? What's wrong?"

"You have to do a search for the purse—maybe in the tunnels, maybe in the men's room—*right now*," Bethany babbled.

"Marigold's purse?" Charley asked, confusion spreading across her face. "Jen has it, right?"

"No, not that purse, the other one. The black one that was Jen's, the one that they swapped. *The one that the killer stole.* Come on!"

She grabbed Charley's arm and pulled her toward the stationmaster's office. Charley dug in her heels and peeled Bethany's fingers from her arm. "You can't drag an on-duty police officer. And the killer is in jail, so not like we have to run to collect evidence."

"See, I'm not totally, one-hundred-percent sure that Ben's the killer." Bethany shrugged apologetically. "I was just talking to Trevor, and he was acting weird. I asked him if Ben had the purse when Trevor saw him come out of the men's room, and—"

"Trevor saw Ben Kovac exit the men's room at the time of the murder?"

"Yeah, at eleven on the dot, so five minutes after the murder. Trevor says there's a maintenance tunnel entrance in the men's room that Ben could have used to access the platform without being seen." Bethany could see Charley mentally running through the timeline. "Anyway, I asked him if Ben had the purse, because obviously the killer would have the purse right after the murder, and Trevor said no. But then he acted weird and left really quickly, so I think he might know something. Maybe where the purse is..."

"Well, come on!" Charley said, this time grabbing Bethany by the arm. "Where is he?"

"Ben's office, because he's filling in as stationmaster for the rest of the day. But maybe he went wherever the purse is, which is probably the maintenance tunnels or the men's room!"

They jogged together across the concourse.

"Men's room first? It's on the way," Bethany suggested.

Charley nodded and banged three times on the restroom door with her fist. "Police, anybody in there?" When no answer came, Charley pushed open the door with one hand and shone her flashlight into the dark restroom with the other. She clicked off the flashlight and flipped the light switch. "Come on in. Let's see this tunnel access point."

Bethany looked around. She'd never been in the men's restroom before and was surprised to see that it was slightly different than the women's. The women's restroom was all one room, with a single toilet, a sink, and a baby changing station.

The men's room was slightly larger, and the toilet was separated from a sink and urinal by a stall. "I don't see a tunnel."

Charley scanned the ceiling and then pushed open the door to the stall. "In here."

Bethany stuck her head into the stall and sure enough, there was a half-size access door in the wall to the left of the toilet.

"Locked," Charley said, jiggling the knob. "Who has keys?"

"Ben, obviously, and Trevor, who is the substitute Ben. He's probably in the stationmaster's office."

"Lead the way."

Bethany knocked at the door to Ben's office, but no one answered. She put her ear to the door. It was so quiet inside, she could hear the desk clock ticking. She shook her head. "Maybe he's in the maintenance closet?"

She led Charley back past the restrooms and knocked on the door. No one answered, but she heard a muffled *bang* like someone running into furniture and an *ouch*, followed by a curse. She nodded toward the door, and Charley rapped on it with her knuckles. "Open up! Police!" More bumping, and then Trevor opened the door, still wearing the stationmaster's cap.

"Yeah?"

"Sir, as the temporary stationmaster, we need your permission to search the maintenance tunnel that leads to the men's room for a piece of evidence related to the murder here earlier this week," Charley said.

"And your keys," added Bethany. Charley shot her a clear don't-interfere-in-my-investigation look.

"Uh, sure," Trevor said, stepping out into the hall and quickly closing the door to the maintenance closet behind him. "Happy to open that up for you."

He seemed too eager to help. Bethany narrowed her eyes. "Why don't we—I mean you, officer—search the maintenance closet, first? Since you're already here."

Charley looked at her quizzically, and Bethany gave her a meaningful I-know-something-so-just-trust-me nod. "Is that all right with you, sir?"

Trevor looked a little panicked. "I don't know, I'll have to ask the ZamRail office what they want me to do."

"I can assure you that ZamRail offered us their full cooperation in this investigation," Charley said, sounding every bit the bored professional. Bethany was impressed with her acting skills. If she didn't know her friend, she'd have thought Charley didn't care whether or not she got inside that maintenance closet. "If you delay the search, I'll just have to close off the area until we can get a team out here to tear it apart. Might have to close the station for a few hours, keep the station employees here for questioning. Could run us until ten p.m., midnight."

Trevor reflexively glanced at his watch. Bethany could tell he was thinking about the imminent delivery of his first child. If he missed it, he'd suffer worse consequences than a police search. "Fine, search the closet. You have my permission." He unlocked the door and propped it open. He hadn't been alone in there—Caboose was walking up and down the workbench, and his purr was so loud that Bethany could hear it from the door.

"Should I expect to find any weapons, drugs, guns, explosives, or other illegal or dangerous items in my search?" Charley asked, donning a pair of latex gloves from a pouch on her belt.

Trevor shook his head. "Nope. Just a set of claws." He nodded at Caboose, who working on the edge of an already-shredded cardboard box.

Charley gingerly picked up the cat and held him out to Trevor. "You two stay right here in the hallway. I'll have one eye on you."

He took the cat and she moved into the maintenance room and began methodically looking into each box on the shelves, even ones that looked slightly too small to hide a purse inside. She tipped each one toward herself, riffling the contents slightly to see what lay underneath, before returning it to its place. Trevor relaxed a bit as he stood beside Bethany and absentmindedly stroked Caboose. *Charley wasn't looking in the right place.*

"Try the workbench," Bethany suggested. Charley shot her another one of those don't-interfere looks, but Bethany saw Trevor's eye twitch. She was getting warmer. She scanned the workbench to see where a purse might be stashed. A plain utility table with a few clamps attached and a bare bulb hanging above, it didn't afford too many hiding places. Except... "The waste basket! Under the bench!"

Trevor groaned, and Charley whipped her head around. "Don't you move, sir." She went over to the waste basket and slid it out. A brown paper bag, clearly full of something, was crammed on top. She opened it gingerly, peered inside, and then closed it again. "We got it," she said, standing up and plucking the bag out of the trash. "It's in here." Bethany grinned exultantly and tried to keep her fist-pump to a minimum.

"I found that!" Trevor yelped, and Caboose jumped out of his arms and streaked down the hall. "I swear! It's not what it looks like."

"Well, it looks like the purse that Marigold had on the morning she was killed. Are you telling me it's a different purse?" Charley frowned.

"No, but—"

"Are you telling me you found a valuable handbag in your workplace, and you did not turn it in the Lost and Found or report it to the police?"

"Well, yes, but—"

"I think you might be in a lot of trouble, Mr. MacDonald. I suggest you come down to the station with me and call a lawyer so we can sort this out."

"Please, just hear me out. I can explain what happened. I just can't go to the station and deal with this tonight, because then there's no way I can make it to the hospital. My wife's like five centimeters already, see?" He held out his phone, and Charley took a step back.

"Enough," Charley said. "You have three minutes to give me an explanation of why you have this purse. Convince me that you did not grab it off Marigold's arm before you pushed her onto those tracks, or so help me God, I am taking you downtown, and you will have to answer to a grand jury *and* your wife. Time starts now."

"Um, OK." Trevor twisted his hands. "Um, so I was doing my thing, emptying trash cans on Wednesday evening after the murder. They were really full because there were so many people stuck here that day. Super gross, full of food. No offense, Bethany."

"None taken."

"A lot of the cans I had to take the trash out by hand, because they were so over-full that if I just pulled the bag, a bunch would fall on the floor. And like soda and stuff is bad for the marble, and this old place is falling apart as it is..."

Charley motioned with her hand that he should hurry up and get to the point.

Trevor jumped ahead. "OK, OK. In one of the cans I was emptying, I found that purse. I could tell it was fancy because of the logo, and it looked really nice. New, you know? So I put it aside and took it back to the maintenance closet to clean it up a little. I thought it might be something my wife would like, you know, as a push present. Have you heard of those things?"

Charley shook her head.

"Well, it's new. My wife read about it in a magazine. The new mom gets a diamond necklace from her husband after the baby is born or whatever. We don't really have money for jewelry or anything, and it was really stressing me out, so this was like the universe saying, 'Hey, here you go, here's a present Julie will like.'"

"Why didn't you give it to Ben for the Lost and Found?" Bethany interrupted, ignoring Charley's annoyed expression.

"It was in the trash." Trevor shrugged. "Didn't figure anyone was looking for it."

"It could have been stolen," Charley said. "It *was* stolen."

"Plus, were you really going to give your wife a trash purse?" Bethany wrinkled her nose.

"It's nice!" Trevor said indignantly. "I cleaned off all the soup. Anyway, while I was cleaning it, I heard something clunking inside, and it was my keys!"

"Why didn't you turn in the purse at that time?" Charley asked. "You knew it was Marigold's at that point, obviously."

"There was nothing else in it. I didn't think it had evidensary value."

"Evidentiary," Charley corrected.

"Right. I didn't see how finding the empty purse would help the police, and I *did* see how the purse would make my wife happy. Doesn't take a genius to do that math."

"No worries there," Charley muttered. "Especially now that you've cleaned off any fingerprints."

"The purse does have some evidentiary value, though," Bethany said thoughtfully. "It proves one thing—the killer was inside the train station after the murder. It wasn't a random person who ran off before the police locked down the station. It was someone who needed to get rid of that purse to avoid being caught."

Charley nodded. "Good point. Which garbage can did you find it in?"

Trevor hemmed and hawed for a few seconds. "Er...I don't remember," he said. "There are a lot of cans. It was definitely on the concourse. Maybe the one by the ticket booth?"

"Maybe?"

Trevor shrugged. "That's my best guess. If I had to bet money on it, that's what I'd say."

Trevor's mention of betting reminded Bethany of something Ben had said. "Did you really owe Marigold a thousand dollars?"

"What?" Charley said. "Why haven't I heard anything about this? Is it true?"

Trevor took off the stationmaster's cap and crumpled it in his hands. "It was more like twelve hundred dollars, to be honest. We play poker every week, and it adds up."

Charley shook her head. "Your three minutes are definitely up, and you've told me that you have the purse stolen by Marigold's killer, you owed her money, and you hid both these facts from police. I have to say, not very convincing when it comes to your innocence. I think you better come downtown with me."

"Are you arresting me?" Trevor put the cap back on and crossed his arms. "Because if you're not, I have to get back to work."

Bethany turned to Charley and spoke under her breath. "*Can* you arrest him? I mean, if you still have Ben in custody for the same crime?"

"Yeah, it's legal, but not something we want to be doing. It doesn't exactly promote trust with the public if we just arrest everyone involved and sort it out later. I could charge him because he destroyed evidence by cleaning the purse, but it probably wouldn't stick unless he was *trying* to remove the fingerprints. He says he was just cleaning off the soup from the trash, and that's plausible."

"Pretty sure his wife will testify against him if she finds out about the trash purse." Bethany snickered, but Charley didn't laugh at the joke. Instead, she turned back to Trevor.

"Did Marigold ever try to collect on the debt? I mean get the twelve hundred bucks you owed her?"

"Kind of."

"What does that mean?"

"I mean, she told me she'd clear the debt if I gave her my keys so she could get her purse out of Ben's office."

"So *that's* why you loaned her your keys!" Bethany cried. "I couldn't figure out why you'd do that—it was so out of character! I thought maybe it was the stress of the new baby, or all the extra work Ben was having you do."

"You believe him?" From Charley's tone, it was clear she didn't.

"I mean, it makes sense. Marigold would forfeit twelve hundred dollars if it meant she could steal a check worth fifty thousand dollars."

"But this guy!" Charley said. "He had motive, means, and opportunity, just like Ben Kovac, but he has evidence of the crime, too! And he tried to hide it, like an idiot."

"Hey!" Trevor said, waving his hand from the doorway. "Still here—I can hear you."

"Well, really, the trash can? You know every inch of this place. You could have put it behind a heating grate or something."

"I was in a hurry," Trevor mumbled.

Bethany grabbed Charley's arm. Charley shook her off. "I told you not to grab—"

Bethany interrupted her. "Do you trust me?"

"I mean, most of the time."

"Hold off on arresting Trevor. His first child will be born today—he's not going anywhere." She leaned in and murmured in Charley's ear, "I know how to figure out who killed Marigold."

Charley stared into Bethany's eyes like she was searching for something. "Fine," she said. Trevor whooped, and she shot him a cold glare. "Against my better judgment, I'll wait to make an arrest until after his baby is born. But *you* better be local when I come looking for you, Mr. MacDonald."

"I promise!" he said. "On my baby's life. Thank you, Officer Perez. You won't regret this."

"You better have a plan," Charley said to Bethany as they walked back to the Souperb kiosk.

"I do, I swear. By the end of the day tomorrow, whether it's Ben or someone else, we'll remove any doubt about who killed Marigold. At the memorial—"

Before Bethany could finish her sentence, Olive walked over from the bakery and interrupted. "Speaking of the memorial, have you decided what soup you're making? I want to coordinate the menu."

Charley tapped the brown paper bag. "I can't wait around—I need to get this into evidence."

"Go," Bethany said. "We can talk about it tonight."

"Talk about what?" Olive asked after Charley headed out.

Bethany opened her mouth to say *how to catch Marigold's murderer*, but thought better of it. The fewer people who were in on it, the better. "Just our weekend plans," she said breezily.

Olive nodded. "*After* the memorial, I presume. I need all hands on deck to pull it off."

"Of course, Kimmy and Charley and I will be there."

"Did you decide on a soup to serve?" Olive asked. "Were Jen and Aaron any help with ideas of what Marigold would have wanted? I was thinking it should probably be vegetarian, since you never know who will be there. Or maybe two soups, one vegetarian? Or maybe that's too complicated. One soup, no meat. But what about dairy? If someone is lactose intolerant, we still want them to be able to eat it, don't we?"

Bethany grinned at Olive's brimming enthusiasm. "Slow down! I haven't picked a recipe yet, but let's talk about it. Jen said Marigold wouldn't care one way or another. And we know she liked my soups, so we can assume she'd approve of whatever we pick."

Olive sighed. "I just want it to be perfect. I want the family to feel comforted, like Marigold was loved and supported here."

Bethany choked. "Olive, you kinda hated her."

"Well, she was hateful! But I really needed that comfort when my sister died. It was so helpful to have friends, good food, and good memories around me. That's what gave me closure. Plus, it'll make all of us here at the station feel more settled."

I'll feel more settled when I'm sure the murderer is behind bars, Bethany thought, but she just nodded. "You're a good friend, Olive, even to your enemies. What about split pea soup, like she made the day she died, except jazzed up a little so it's more like her? You know, brighter, more fun, less old-fashioned and stodgy." Her mind was buzzing with ideas. "Sort of an end-of-winter, beginning-of-spring taste."

"Hon, you're making my stomach growl. I'll do an herbed bread stick to go with it. And a gluten-free version, of course." Olive sniffed and dabbed her eyes with her sleeve. "For Marigold. I'm getting a little choked up just thinking about it."

Hard to tell whether Olive was serious or joking. Bethany patted her on the arm. "We'll do right by her."

Olive beamed. "Come early to help set up! And bring as many extra hands as you can. Hm, maybe we could ask Ryan to help set up chairs."

Bethany died a little inside. It felt weird—exploitative, maybe—asking him to work for free just because he was living at the shelter. "I'm sure he has better things to do. Seems like Sister Bernadette keeps him pretty busy."

"Nonsense, I think he'd be interested to attend."

"A memorial for someone he's never met?"

"Maybe there's someone here he'd like to see." Olive winked at her. "And you know he'd look good in a suit and tie."

Bethany blushed in spite of herself. "You and Kimmy have to stop trying to find me dates. Anyway, there's someone else I'm kind of interested in…"

"Ooh, young love!" Olive clasped her hands eagerly. "Tell me more! What's he like? What does he do for a living? Short or tall?"

"I'm not saying a word. It's not even a thing yet, just an idea of a thing. If I talk about it, I'll jinx it. Plus, I don't want you inviting him to a funeral! There's low potential for romance, especially when I'll be running the food services table!"

"Fine." Olive shrugged. "Have it your way. Soup du boring."

Bethany giggled. "You'd prefer 'soup dude bro'?"

"I'd prefer to see all you girls married and settled before—" Olive broke off. "Well, sooner rather than later."

Bethany looked at her friend with concern. Was this about Garrett's health complaints, or was something else weighing on Olive? "Is everything OK? You can tell me if it's not. You know

I'm always on your side." *Like if you pushed Marigold onto the tracks...*

Olive shook her head, silver hair flying around her head like a halo. "It's nothing. Don't you worry about a thing."

• • • •

BETHANY BIKED HOME in the chilly February rain. What was merely a sprinkle at Newbridge Station transformed into a downpour as she rode through Newbridge's charming brick-fronted streets. The weather got so bad that Bethany could hardly see the road in front of her, so she ducked under the awning of the public library to wait it out.

When she peeled back the dripping hood of her jacket, she saw someone else was sheltering there with her. Of course, she had to run into the guy she had a crush on when she looked like a drowned rat.

"What are *you* doing here?" she asked, trying fruitlessly to dry her dripping face by waving her hands in front of it.

Milo pointed up at the sign above the door. "Last time I checked, this was a public place."

"Checking out some weekend reading?" Bethany wondered what kind of books Milo read. She secretly hoped it was cookbooks and travel guides like she preferred, but it was probably the usual guy stuff: thrillers or fantasy novels with swords or something.

"Background research for Marigold Wonder's profile, actually. Just waiting for the rain to chill out before I walk back to the office to write it up."

"I thought the library only had biographies of, you know, famous people."

Milo grinned. "Well, they don't have a biography of Marigold, but they have all kinds of stuff on microfiche that has never been digitized. Plus, there is a global conspiracy of librarians that will work together to hunt down the tiniest little thing. Librarians are my secret weapon when it comes to good reporting."

"Find anything interesting?" Bethany smoothed the wet hair out of her face and tried to look less like a sodden Irish setter and more like *Singing in the Rain*.

"Maybe. I found an article in a Santa Cruz paper about her smoothie shop. Looks like it's still open. The article even has a recent quote from her—did she travel back and forth often?"

"Not that I know of. Maybe she did the interview by video chat or something. I'm sure if you call the shop, the staff will tell you what her habits were."

Milo nodded. "I called them as soon as I read the article. It was obvious the manager didn't know she'd passed away, and I didn't have the heart to tell him. He said she was very involved in the business."

"Huh. I guess that explains how she was able to live on almost no income here in Newbridge," Bethany said. "I wonder why she never mentioned that she still had her old shop. She always talked about her life in California like it was something in the past."

"It's strange. I've done a ton of research for this piece, maybe more than I've ever done before, but I still don't really have a sense who Marigold was. Nobody I've talked to seems to have a very full picture of her life, even though she's always described as outgoing and chatty."

That's putting it mildly. I'd say more like overbearing and bossy. Bethany rolled her eyes. "Wish I could help. All I know about Marigold is that she had sticky fingers."

"What do you mean?" Milo took out his notebook.

"Off the record," she said firmly, flipping the cover of the notebook closed. He grudgingly put it away. "The police think the motive for her murder was because she stole fifty thousand dollars."

"From Ben Kovac? I heard he was arrested this morning."

Bethany shook her head. "Well, sort of. From Newbridge Station's historic restoration fund. Ben administers it, and she stole it from his office, but it wasn't *his* money, per se."

"What'd she need the money for?"

"That's the fifty thousand dollar question."

The rain slowed to a steady light drizzle, and Milo put his hand out to test it. "Looks like my cue to get back to work. I'll see you at the memorial tomorrow?"

Bethany gave a nod. "Yep. I'm catering. Well, Olive and I are working together on it."

"Soup?"

"Of course."

"What kind, if I may ask?"

Bethany laughed. "I thought you needed to get to work."

"This *is* work. I'm talking to a chef who I'm going to write about in the Sunday food feature."

Bethany gasped. "You are? Oh no, I have to totally rethink the menu!"

"Why, are you making something spicy?"

"No, it's pea soup again!"

Milo put his hand to his chest in mock horror. "Not soup of the yesterday!"

She made a face at him. "Never. This is a different pea soup. Lighter, brighter."

"Then you have nothing to fear. I will be there to taste it with an open mind." He smiled at her, his eyes twinkling underneath the brim of his baseball cap.

"I've heard that one before." Bethany crossed her arms. "You're five and zero with the soup tasting, buddy, so I'll believe it when I see it."

"Fair enough." Milo tipped his baseball cap and stepped out onto the sidewalk. "Ms. Bradstreet."

"Mr. Armstrong," Bethany said primly. She swung her leg over Daisy's seat and pushed off into the rain. She hardly felt the cold drops against her face on the way home. She was too busy thinking about what Milo Armstrong would say when he tried her soup tomorrow.

• • • •

"WHAT IN JACQUES PEPIN'S name are you doing?" Kimmy stood in the middle of the kitchen gaping at the mess, still wearing her Café Sabine chef's jacket.

Bethany looked around. Dozens of crumpled pieces of yellow paper were strewn around the main room of their apartment. Dirty dishes filled the sink and covered the counters, and the wastebasket at her feet was overflowing with even more pieces of paper. "Recipe testing. And also solving a murder." She put her head down and continued scribbling on the legal pad.

"I hope you're going to wash these pots and pans before you go on ahead with your crime-solving."

Bethany grinned wickedly. "Oh yeah, dishes are way more important than murdered people. I'll get right on that."

"What if Charley said that? 'Oh no, can't brush my teeth because I gotta solve crimes. Can't sweep the floor because I gotta solve crimes'? She'd never get anything done."

"Speaking of, she'll be here in a few minutes."

"To do the dishes?"

Bethany cackled. "Nope. To solve crimes."

Kimmy sighed and stomped off to take a shower. When she came back out in her bathrobe and hair wrap, she was in a better mood—probably because Bethany had scrubbed the biggest pots and picked up the paper on the floor. "Better," she said.

Bethany curtsied. "Sorry you had to come home to a mess after you just finished cleaning up a mess at work."

Kimmy raised her head haughtily. "You are forgiven! Arise, fair subject, and avenge our fallen friend—er, something like that."

"Our fallen non-friend, but it doesn't matter if we liked her, does it? It matters that people don't push other people in front of trains for money. Don't get me wrong, I would do a lot of things for fifty K. That's enough money to open a restaurant."

"A very small one," Kimmy said wryly. "I'd say 250 K would give you a better start."

"Well, it'd cover one that had, you know, doors?"

"I know, sorry."

"But I wouldn't kill for it, not even someone I didn't like." Bethany stabbed the legal pad with her pencil for emphasis. "The question is, who *would*?"

A knock came at the door, and Kimmy went to answer it. When Charley entered the living room, Bethany was shocked at the dark circles under her friend's eyes.

"You look exhausted! Are you sick or something?"

Charley sprawled on the couch. "Just a long day. The chief was putting pressure on me to arrest Trevor at the hospital. I had to convince her that he's not a flight risk. Basically, I am going to lose my job if Trevor skips town."

"He won't," Bethany said, only seventy-five percent sure but putting one-hundred-percent certainty into her voice. "He loves his family too much."

"So lay this genius plan of yours on me. I swear, Bethany, if this is something stupid, I am firing you as Kimmy's roommate." Charley grabbed one of the throw pillows and put it over her face. "I'm just resting this here while I listen."

Bethany cleared her throat and organized the papers in front of her. "Part one of the plan is...let Ben out of jail."

"*What?*" Charley sat up so fast that the throw pillow flew across the room. Even Kimmy looked rattled. "I can't let someone charged with murder *out of jail*. That is not a thing, Bethany. He's being held without bail."

"OK, you don't like part one. I will just put a question mark by it, and we can come back to it."

"Fine." Charley lay back down, and Kimmy retrieved the throw pillow and gently put it back over Charley's face.

"Part two. Since we know the murderer killed Marigold because of the money—"

Charley sat up again, the pillow falling into her lap this time. "Do we know that, Bethany? Do we?"

"Well, the killer took her purse before pushing her onto the tracks, right? And the purse is the logical place for the money. We know the killer went through the purse, because Marigold's wallet wasn't inside it when Trevor found it. And Marigold must have known that someone wanted the check, or she wouldn't have stuffed it into her bra."

"OK, go on." Charley lay back down on the couch and put the pillow over her face.

Bethany scanned her notes to find her place. "Ah, yes. Since we know the murderer killed Marigold because of the money and *did not get the money*, the murderer is still motivated to get the check."

"Yeah, but the check is in evidence," Charley said through the pillow.

"That brings me to part three, get the check out of evidence."

This time Charley rolled off the couch onto the floor and lay there pretending to be dead.

"It doesn't have to be the real check. Just look enough like the real check for the murderer to believe it's real."

"Phew." Charley crawled back onto the couch, but stayed propped up on her elbows, watching Bethany with more interest. "I kind of see where you're going with this."

"I don't," Kimmy said. She sat down on the floor and crossed her legs. "You're going to use the check to bait the murderer into what? Confessing?"

"You do get it!" Bethany high-fived her.

"Why would the murderer confess?"

"Well, not confess, but expose him or herself by trying to steal the check again," Charley explained.

"But why does Ben need to be released from jail?" Kimmy looked at Bethany.

"Because he didn't do it," Bethany said, crossing her arms and glaring at Charley.

Charley threw the pillow at her. "You don't know that. You just want it to be true."

"I *know*-know. It's all about the purse." Bethany tried to keep a smug expression off her face, but Kimmy saw it and pointed at her.

Charley, irritated, said, "How do you figure? Ben could just have easily snatched it, taken out the wallet, and dumped the purse and keys before someone saw him with it."

"No way. First of all, Ben would never in a million years dump those keys in a trash can. Those keys are like diamonds to him. He'd immediately recognize them."

Charley nodded. "Fair point. But I also think it's possible that Trevor was lying about the keys being in the purse. If he was the murderer, he'd want us to think he didn't have his keys that day, because it would mean he wasn't on the platform at 10:55. So we have to believe Trevor if we consider the keys as evidence of Ben's innocence, and I don't think I can believe Trevor at this point."

"OK, fine. Question mark by the keys. Second, why would Ben carry the purse all the way out to the ticket office trash can where he might be seen? He'd have gone straight back to his office to look through the purse, and then disposed of it from there."

Charley tilted her head thoughtfully. "Maybe. But maybe he was also smart enough not to keep the purse in his office, you know? There were cops all over Newbridge Station that day. He'd have wanted the purse as far away from himself as possible. Something that size isn't easy to hide...you saw what a bad job Trevor did."

Bethany nodded. "Fair point. Third, Ben thought Trevor was doing the maintenance rounds that day. He'd have been sure to run into Trevor on the platform or in the tunnels on a normal day. So if Ben *were* the killer, I don't think he would have taken the purse at all. It was too likely he'd be seen with it. He could have just left the purse with Marigold's body, waited for the police to recover the check, and the check would have been put back in the historic restoration fund. Only someone who wanted the check for themselves would have taken the purse."

"Hm." Charley sat still on the couch, and Bethany waited with her heart in her throat. "Hm."

"He totally didn't do it!" Kimmy blurted out. "You know he didn't, Charley. You have to let him go!"

Finally, Charley nodded. "You're right. I have to go file another report after midnight. Thanks a lot, Bethany. Why can't we have these conversations at three in the afternoon?"

"Because I do my best thinking with Kimmy around." Bethany grinned. "Wait, one more question before you go. Something's been bothering me. Did Jen's fiancé have a ticket for the 10:55 train? I mean, did someone see the ticket to confirm it?"

Charley frowned. "I don't remember. I don't think I interviewed him. I'll look up his statement while I'm there."

After Charley left, Kimmy picked at the stitches in the throw pillow and was uncharacteristically quiet. Bethany went to the freezer to investigate the ice cream situation. "We've got chocolate and chocolate," she reported.

"Chocolate for me," Kimmy said.

Bethany scooped them both a serving and returned to the couch where Kimmy had nearly picked a hole in the pillow. "Is something bothering you?" Bethany asked, handing her a bowl and spoon.

"I was just thinking about who might have done it. You know, pushed her. If it's not Ben"—Kimmy shoveled in a huge bite of ice cream—"then who? Augh, brain freeze!"

"I know. That's why I'm trying not to think about it too much. No point in driving ourselves crazy—it'll all come out tomorrow." Bethany looked over and saw Kimmy's eyes welling up with tears. "What? Ice cream headache? Or something else? You have to tell me what you're thinking."

Kimmy kept her eyes on her bowl. "What if it's Olive?" she said, her voice cracking when she said Olive's name.

"Olive couldn't kill someone!"

"I don't know," Kimmy said. "She's soft on the outside, but the woman is made of steel. But she doesn't have an alibi, does she? And Bethany—she really needs money right now."

Bethany rolled her eyes. "What are you talking about? The Honor Roll is doing great!"

"But Garrett isn't doing great."

"She said he wasn't feeling well, but I don't know what's going on—do you?"

Kimmy nodded slowly. "He has liver cancer, and he needs surgery. Their health insurance only covers part of the cost. It's going to run them thousands of dollars, and I don't think they have it. All their money is in the bakery and their house."

Bethany stirred her ice cream until it started to soften. She took a bite and savored the creamy chill on her tongue, considering the new information. Could Olive be the murderer? *I mean, she didn't like Marigold, but would she kill her for money?* It seemed preposterous. But then, Olive herself said that desperate people do stupid things—and finding out that your husband was dying would make a person pretty desperate. "When did they learn about Garrett's cancer?"

"Last week."

"That's enough time to freak out and decide to do something drastic, I guess. How would Olive know Marigold had the money, though?"

"Maybe she told her she had a windfall coming. Bragged about it. The woman had a big mouth."

Bethany nodded as she scraped the last few drops of ice cream from her bowl. That seemed entirely in character for Marigold, who'd even blabbed about Ben's poker-game proposal. Bethany stopped with her spoon in her mouth. "Wait—Garrett knew about the restoration fund donation. Maybe he and Olive figured out that Marigold had taken it."

"Garrett did? How?"

"He was at the poker game on Monday night when Ben told everyone about it."

Kimmy paused with her spoon in her mouth. "So Garrett found out at the same time as Marigold and Trevor."

"And Jen, too. She had just come into town that afternoon. Marigold said she came with her to the poker game. I remember because she called her a party pooper for not gambling."

Bethany made a face at Marigold's choice of words. "What do you think Marigold was going to do with that money, anyway? She had to know she'd get caught if she was flashing it around."

Kimmy cleared their dishes to the sink and rinsed out the bowls, stacking them neatly on the counter. Over her shoulder, she said, "She probably just assumed Ben wouldn't turn her in to protect his job. I doubt she told Olive that she was going to steal it. Probably just said she was going to inherit some cash or something."

"You're talking like Olive did it. Like it isn't even a question."

Kimmy smoothed her head wrap with her hands. "Everything points to her. I just can't figure out who else it could be."

"I can help you there," Bethany said. "Basically anyone who was in the station and wasn't a passenger on the 10:55 is potentially the killer. So I'll start listing people, and you can tell me why each person isn't the murderer."

"I don't know if I like this game," Kimmy said warily as she plopped down on the floor next to Bethany.

"You can quit any time." Kimmy nodded, and Bethany began. "Me."

"I quit!"

Bethany laughed. "You can't quit before you even start. Anyway, I gave you an easy one first."

"OK, you didn't do it because you were at Café Sabine, plus you're a decent human who wouldn't murder someone. Next."

Bethany paused. "The weird thing is, this whole situation has made me realize that decent people can commit murder under the right circumstances. Who do we know that *isn't* decent? Nobody. And someone we know did this."

"I don't want to play this game," Kimmy said, pouting.

"You don't have to if it's stressing you out. I just thought it would be an interesting exercise. We can call it a night."

Kimmy swatted her on the arm. "No, I can't sleep now! I'll be thinking about this all night if we don't lay it all out. Next suspect!"

"OK, Garrett."

"Working the counter at the Honor Roll. Too easy. Next!"

"Jen Smith."

"The cousin? In the bathroom, then working in Marigold's booth. Next."

Bethany shook her head. "I didn't see her come out of the bathroom. And I didn't notice when she got back to split pea central. She probably had a couple of minutes between the bathroom and the kiosk to run down to the platform and push Marigold."

"I guess so. I haven't met her—from what you've said, she doesn't have enough backbone to be a murderer, but people who are family have a whole lifetime of reasons to kill each other. She's a question mark. Next?"

"Aaron."

Kimmy tilted her head questioningly. "That's the crabby fiancé? He was on the train."

Bethany held up a finger. "Not so fast. Charley is still checking on that one. He may have just pretended to be a passenger to avoid real scrutiny."

"Isn't that why Marigold was on the platform, though? To meet his train?"

Bethany nodded. "Yeah. Or at least, that's what Jen said. But they could both be lying. Aaron could have been in town the whole time and just not come to the station before that morning."

"Well, Marigold was on the platform for *some* reason," Kimmy said. "If it wasn't to meet that guy's train, then why was she down there?"

"Let's see. She could have been meeting someone else who was on the 10:55 train. Or she could have been lured there by the murderer for some reason other than meeting the train." Bethany drummed her fingers on the coffee table while they thought.

"Question mark by the crabby fiancé, then. At least until Charley checks on his ticket. Next suspect."

"Trevor."

"Um. Too dumb?" Kimmy grinned.

"Well, he did get caught with the purse," Bethany said. "But Trevor isn't dumb. He can fix pretty much anything, and he knows the ins and outs of the train station like no one else, not even Ben. He owed Marigold money, and she clearly needed money or she wouldn't have stolen the check from Ben's office. Maybe she saw him on his rounds, tried to hold his keys hostage to collect the money he owed her, and the conversation went south. He's a big guy—he wouldn't even have to push her very hard."

"It sounds plausible when you put it that way. I'd give Trevor more than a question mark on your little list. Who's left? Ben?"

Bethany nodded. "What do you think about him?"

"I think...I think Ben had the hots for her, and that's always a good motive to kill someone."

"It is? Planning to kill Charley anytime soon?"

"No, of course not." Kimmy rolled her eyes. "Charley's too tough to kill, plus she has a gun and a Taser and stuff. She's a black belt in karate, did you know that?"

Bethany nodded. "Yup. But you're supposed to be telling me why Ben *didn't* do it."

"Oh yeah. He didn't do it because the check led back to him. It's too obvious. And he's a principled person—principled enough that he didn't give Marigold the money, even though he knew she'd report him to his superiors and he'd probably lose his job. If he was the kind of person who'd murder someone, he'd just give her the cash out of the restoration fund. No skin off his teeth, right? It wasn't even his money." Kimmy stifled a huge yawn. "Next suspect."

"Ummm"—Bethany checked her list—"I think that's it."

Kimmy snapped her fingers. "Wrong! You missed one."

Bethany ran down the list: herself, Olive, Garrett, Jen, Aaron, Trevor, Ben. "That's everyone."

"One more person was there. You saw him right after the train came in, remember?"

Bethany thought back. Right after the 10:55 arrived, Milo showed up at the kiosk to taste the soup for the food feature. He'd seemed—normal. Definitely not like he'd just killed someone. "So is it my turn to say why he didn't do it?"

Kimmy nodded.

"OK, one, he would have had to run from the platform to the kiosk, but he wasn't out of breath at all."

"Maybe he's in really good shape from running marathons or something."

"He does ride his bike a lot." Bethany drummed her fingers on the coffee table, thinking. "Two, he had no motive to hurt Marigold."

Kimmy cocked her head to the side. "You know him so well? Maybe he and Marigold were having a"—she wiggled her finger around—"thing. And he found out that Ben proposed or something. Maybe it wasn't about the money at all, and she had some kind of love note from him in her purse, so he took the purse to hide evidence of their relationship. Or maybe he knew about the money and wanted it—I don't think newspaper reporters are exactly rolling in the dough."

"I thought we were talking about why he *didn't* do it." Bethany glared at Kimmy, surprised that her heart was beating so fast. Kimmy's idea was silly, right? Milo and Marigold? *Oh no, even their names sounded good together!* "A secret relationship might explain how Marigold got him to come down to the station for a food feature when I've been open for months without any interest from the paper."

"And you have to admit, a train station murder is a pretty juicy story for an aspiring crime reporter."

"You're not suggesting he committed a crime so he'd have something to write about?!"

"You're the one who doesn't like to rule out possibilities."

Bethany sighed. "I guess it's possible. If he thought the story would be a career-maker *and* he was completely amoral and evil, murder could be a logical choice. A career is worth more than fifty thousand dollars."

"See?" Kimmy said. "You can't rule him out."

Bethany shook her head. "You just don't want it to be Olive."

"*You* just don't want it to be Milo." Kimmy crossed her arms and scowled.

"I guess we both have our blind spots," Bethany snapped. She looked at the clock. Almost 1:30. Maybe she was feeling so annoyed because she was tired. "I'd better go to bed. I have to get up in five hours to make Marigold's memorial soup."

"Guess that means I have to get up in five hours, too," Kimmy grumbled.

Bethany sighed. "I'm sorry. Maybe I should start looking for another place to cook. I don't want to be a hassle for you like this. I know it's a big risk for you to let me use the café kitchen."

"It's not a hassle! I'm just tired." Kimmy gave her a sympathetic smile.

"It *is* a hassle. You have to open early for me all the time, and you work late almost every night. You taste my soups and give me pointers and show me new techniques. You order ingredients for me, and you never complain about any of it. You've done so much to help me get Souperb going. I'll never be able to pay you back for all that."

"I said it's not a hassle!"

"Thanks, Kimmy." Bethany said. "But if it ever is a problem for you, you'll tell me, right? I don't want to take advantage of you just because you were trying to help out a friend. Any time, you can kick me out of your kitchen—no hard feelings."

Kimmy nodded and yawned. "G'night."

"Night."

After Kimmy closed the door to her bedroom, Bethany's stomach was still in knots. Her list of suspects had more question marks than anything else, and she had to make sure all of them knew that the check was still up for grabs at the memorial. There was no way around it—tomorrow she had to lie to all her friends. And worse, by the end of the day, they would know she'd lied to them because she thought they were capable of murder.

Chapter 9

Bethany deglazed the stock pot where she'd been sautéing ramps with an entire bottle of pinot grigio.

"Wow!" Charley said as she was hit with the cloud of wine-steam. "Can I taste it yet?"

"Ew, no, it's just hot wine right now," Kimmy said.

"How much longer until I can have some?" Charley asked, leaning against the counter opposite the range.

Bethany added a couple gallons of vegetable broth, stirred the soup, turned the flame down, and put the lid back on the pot. "Did you skip breakfast this morning or something?"

"As a matter of fact, I did. I was too busy doing stuff like letting your friend out of jail."

Kimmy swooped in, gave Charley a peck on the cheek, and handed her a croissant. "For that, you get a snack to tide you over."

"Fifteen minutes, tops," Bethany added. She went to the walk-in and stared at the selection of fresh herbs. *Mint, definitely. Maybe some rosemary or thyme?*

"Tarragon," Kimmy said from behind her. She handed Bethany a large, stainless-steel bowl of fresh peas. Bethany dumped them in the pot along with a bundle of tarragon and mint.

She tasted the soup after it'd simmered for a few minutes. Good, but something was missing. She grabbed another spoon and offered it to Kimmy.

"Hey!" Charley protested.

"It's not there yet. I need a professional palate," Bethany explained.

Kimmy tasted the broth and rolled it around on her tongue. "More salt. I like the herbs, though. Maybe a bit of cream when you blend it?"

Bethany giggled. "You always say cream. You're right about the salt, though." She added a bit, tasted again with a clean spoon, and smacked her lips. "Better!" She fished out the bundle of herbs, moved the pot off the heat, and used the café's giant immersion blender to emulsify the soup. She ladled out a couple of small bowls and handed them to Kimmy and Charley, watching them closely as they tried the finished soup for the first time.

"I'd put in some cream, but it's good," Kimmy said, closing her eyes. "Really good."

"Add some bacon and it'd be perfect." Charley grinned.

"I thought you were going to say chili peppers. Maybe I'll make a bacon garnish, so people who want it can add it, but the vegans can skip it. Bacon crumble? Bacon breadcrumbs?"

"Breadcrumbs," Kimmy and Charley said together.

Bethany nodded. "Breadcrumbs it is. And I'll use gluten-free bread, for Marigold."

* * * *

THE POT OF SOUP WAS so heavy that it took all three of them to haul it over to Newbridge Station. Bethany gasped when she saw how Olive had transformed the concourse for the memorial.

The benches in the passenger waiting area were arranged so they faced the archway over the platform entrance, where a large sign on an easel proclaimed, "In Memory of Marigold" in curly script. Each bench was decorated with a nosegay of marigolds, and arrangements of marigolds and gerbera daisies brightened the food service table. Olive had set up a warmer on a long table in the back for serving food that was already stocked with bowls, spoons, and bread plates. Another station to the right of the benches had coffee, tea, and lemon water.

"Don't forget to give me the signal," Charley said through her teeth as they heaved the pot onto the warmer. "I'm going to circulate and keep an eye on everyone, but I'll be watching for your sign."

Bethany nodded and searched the small crowd to see who'd already arrived. Olive was bustling around welcoming people to the memorial. She saw Bethany and gave her a thumb's up. Trevor was there, too, beaming in a light pink button-up shirt. He stopped by the table as Bethany was writing "Spring Pea with Bacon Breadcrumbs" on her chalk board.

"It's a girl!" he said, cheeks as pink as his shirt. "We named her Olivia. Eight pounds. Want to see a picture?" He pulled out his phone.

"Congratulations!" Bethany and Kimmy said together, leaning to see the photo of the red-faced newborn with a tuft of blonde hair.

"Olivia is a great name," Bethany added. "Olive must be thrilled."

"Julie and I had our first date at the Honor Roll." Trevor beamed. "Do you need any help? Don't let this get-up fool you...I can still lend a hand with anything you need." He pointed to the keys attached to his belt.

"Oh, Trevor!" Olive interrupted, Jen and Aaron in tow. "Could you be a dear and wheel over the cart of breadsticks from the bakery? And tell Garrett to get off his keister and come help, too. You didn't need him, did you?" she asked Bethany, as Trevor left for the Honor Roll. Bethany shook her head.

"We decided to serve food first, then have the service, so people can grieve on a full stomach," Olive said to Jen.

"Everyone in Newbridge is so thoughtful," Jen murmured.

Aaron rolled his eyes. "The Newbridge cops very thoughtfully released the prime suspect for the memorial, too."

"Ah!" Olive clasped her hands as Garrett and Trevor wheeled the bakery cart to the table. "Put the breadsticks in these baskets. The ones in the green bin are the gluten-free. Garrett, will you serve? I want to be able to chat with people." Garrett grumbled as he rolled up his sleeves and took his place behind the bread station, but Olive ignored him.

"Just perfect!" she said, straightening the tablecloth and moving the cutlery around. She turned to Jen. "What do you think? Would Marigold approve?"

Jen nodded. "I'm sure she'd be thrilled with all the attention."

Aaron stiffened as Ben walked over with tears in his eyes. He put one arm around Olive and the other around Trevor. "Things look great, you two. You really pulled it off."

"Ben!" Olive squealed, turning and grabbing his face with two hands. "Now this is just the icing on the cake."

Ben's eyes were tired, but they were glowing. "It's thanks to Bethany. She convinced the police that I was innocent. They even gave me back the check for the restoration fund." Bethany smiled, but inside she was tense, watching the faces of the people standing by the food service table. She couldn't help feeling guilty that Ben thought he was off the hook, too—there was a chance he'd be arrested again if her plan didn't work.

"Really?" Trevor asked. He seemed surprised that the money had been returned so soon. Jen was near tears and Aaron glared at Ben, but that was to be expected—they still thought he was the killer. Olive looked overjoyed, while Garrett wore a dour expression...the usual. Bethany sighed. No indication any of them were especially interested in the money. *Maybe this trap idea is stupid.*

Ben nodded. "The check is in my office right now. I'm going to deposit it right after the memorial, and then we can start planning the restoration. This place is going to get the facelift it needs and deserves."

"Bravo!" Olive said, clapping her hands. "Oh, look, people are really filing in. I'd better go be the welcoming committee and let them know to come get some food."

"I think we're going to get a rush. Do you mind helping me?" Bethany asked Kimmy.

Kimmy shook her head. "I'd rather serve than mingle—I'm a back of the house girl."

Bethany took her place behind the food service table, elbow-to-elbow with Kimmy, and set out the dishes of bacon breadcrumbs. On the other side, Garrett slouched at his station, his eyes resigned and his tongs poised to distribute Olive's fragrant herbed breadsticks. Bethany wanted to say something to him, offer him some kind of condolences about his cancer diagnosis, but she wasn't sure what to say. It seemed cruel to bring it up, especially at what amounted to a funeral, so instead she stood beside him and served soup as she watched New-bridge residents offer Jen and Aaron their condolences before coming over to partake of the free meal.

Bethany was surprised to see Ryan stride through the door. He actually showed up! And he must have hit the shelter's wardrobe closet—his tailored, navy-blue suit fit him perfectly. *Yum.*

Kimmy elbowed her. "You're blushing! Is that the re-porter?"

Bethany felt her cheeks redden even more. "No, that's Ryan—the artist from the shelter." She quickly ladled a bowl of pea soup and handed it to the next person in line. She wasn't the only one who had noticed Ryan come in. Across the room, Olive plucked a marigold from one of the table arrangements and tucked it into Ryan's buttonhole, patting his lapel like a proud mother.

"You didn't tell me he was smoking hot," Kimmy said un-der her breath. "I can't believe you left that out. He makes a girl want to switch teams."

Bethany giggled. "Cute, but not my type." *My type has a paying job.* Speaking of her type, someone was notably ab-sent—Milo-stinking-Armstrong. His promise of a food feature was probably empty, just a nicety to smooth over their awk-ward meeting under the library awning. Or a ploy to dig up dirt for his story on Marigold's murder.

That's it, no more flirting with reporters. They only wanted one thing: column inches. Milo would come when he heard Ben had been released from jail, and she wouldn't let him bail on the food feature again—not after he'd been stringing her along all week.

She quickly ladled some soup into a small pot and ran over to her kiosk to put it on the warmer there. She wasn't going to miss out on a review just because he was late. When he showed, he'd have no excuse not to try her cooking. As the line for soup grew longer, she scanned the crowd to see if he had arrived. *No such luck.*

"Still looking for Milo?" Kimmy asked, handing a bowl of soup to an elderly woman in a large hat. Bethany nodded. "Don't worry, he won't miss this—not if he gets to see you. Plus, he promised he was writing the food feature about you, didn't he?"

Bethany offered bacon breadcrumbs to the next person in line. "I'm not so sure. I think he was just being nice because he wanted inside info about Marigold for his other article. Or maybe he felt guilty because the head-to-head feature with Marigold was canceled. I doubt he'll follow through, though."

"He'll be here for the memorial even if he's not here for food. He'll want to cover Ben being released from jail, right? Hey, is that him?"

Kimmy was right. Bethany stood on tiptoe to peer over the line of waiting customers and spied Milo near the entrance. He had on a rumpled jacket and tie, she noticed—he looked nice, even if he wasn't quite in the smoking hot category. As she predicted, rather than heading for the food service table, he made a beeline for Ben. He pulled out his notebook, and the two men began an animated conversation.

"Maybe when he's done interviewing Ben, he'd have a few minutes to taste the soup," Kimmy said reassuringly.

Bethany shrugged. "He will or he won't. I'm not going to waste energy worrying about him." It was a lie, but her pride wouldn't let her admit how much she wanted that food feature. Kimmy didn't say anything, but her look was knowing.

Now that she wasn't on the lookout for Milo, Bethany noticed someone else was missing from the crowd. She gasped. *Of course.*

"Is it time?" Kimmy asked.

Bethany nodded. She caught Charley's attention and flashed her an "OK" sign. "I think so. Can you hold down the fort while I go check?"

"Of course," Kimmy said confidently, in full sous-chef mode. "Go get 'em."

Bethany untied her apron and, after stashing it under the table, walked quickly toward the hall to the stationmaster's office. She checked both restrooms on the way—*empty.*

She put her ear to the door of Ben's office and could hear someone rifling through the desk drawers. *It was really happening.* The killer had taken the bait and was trying to steal the check! She put her hand on the knob and slowly pushed the door open. The figure inside froze. Bethany scanned for a weapon and then breathed a sigh of relief when she didn't see one. She stepped inside the office. "Looking for something?"

Jen straightened, tucking a slip of paper into the purse under her arm. "I just thought I dropped my earring in here." She stepped toward the door, but Bethany blocked her way.

"You dropped your earring inside Ben's desk?"

Jen shrugged, her eyes darting around the room. "Maybe. You never can tell. They were my grandmother's, so I'd hate—"

"You can stop lying. One, you're wearing both earrings. And two, you're in here to steal the restoration fund check. I knew it would be you. Charley—Officer Perez—wasn't sure, so we set a trap. But deep down, I knew you were the only one who could have killed Marigold."

Something in Jen's face changed, and she sighed. "How'd you figure it out?"

Bethany pointed to the sparkly handbag on Jen's arm. "The purse. There just wasn't enough time for you to swap handbags on the morning of the murder. Plus, I know Marigold wouldn't have given away her bedazzled beauty for a plain black bag, no matter what the designer label was inside."

Jen chuckled humorlessly. "I guess you knew her well. But you're wrong—I was in the restroom the whole time. You saw me go in there."

"I think you had Trevor's keys, and you used them to access the maintenance tunnel in the men's room. You went down to the platform, grabbed that purse"—Bethany motioned to the handbag on Jen's arm again—"and pushed Marigold onto the tracks. Then you ran back through the tunnel to the men's room. You realized that having two purses would look suspicious, so you threw away your own purse with Trevor's keys inside, and went back to the kiosk to serve split pea soup. You must have been disappointed when you realized the check wasn't in Marigold's purse."

The corner of Jen's mouth twitched. "That's putting it mildly."

"So this was just about the money? I've been wracking my brain to figure out why someone would kill their own cousin. Fifty thousand dollars doesn't seem worth it. Even if Marigold was obnoxious, she was your family!"

Jen's face slowly turned a dark purple-red. She finally spat out, "She wasn't my family. She was *me*!"

"I don't follow."

"I'm not her cousin, Nancy Drew. I'm Marigold. This purse, with the 'M.W.'? It was mine first. *She* stole it from *me*. Along with my name, my appearance, my credit cards, and my smoothie concept. It's taken me six months to track her down. I wouldn't have known it had happened if she hadn't registered to vote in my name! When I tried to vote in the special election this winter, they wouldn't let me cast my ballot. Then the creditors started calling."

Bethany shook her head. "Wait, what? Is that why she had your social security card in her bra?"

Jen rapped on the desk with her knuckles. "Knock knock, wake up. It's not my social security card!" She pulled the card out of her purse and flicked it toward Bethany. "Look at it—what does it say?"

"Jennifer Smith," Bethany read dutifully.

"Right—*not me*. That was *her* social security card in her bra. She wasn't on that platform to meet Aaron's train. She was making a run for it—with the money she owed me."

"Why did she owe you money?" Bethany glanced toward the door. *Where was Charley?* She hoped her friend was listening to the conversation, because she was already confused.

"She racked up over fifty grand in credit card debt in my name and didn't pay any of it. I've had collections people calling me night and day. I finally got a copy of the charges and noticed most of them were here in Newbridge, and it didn't take long to find her, considering she was using my name! So I came to make her pay her own bills. They're threatening to take my business!"

Realization dawned on Bethany. "So you told her she needed to give you fifty grand—"

"Fifty-three, to be exact."

"And you were there when Ben said he'd gotten the donation to the restoration fund in almost that exact amount. So you told her to get that money any way she could, or you'd expose her whole deal and send her to jail."

"Bingo. If she went to jail, I'd still have to untangle the whole mess." Jen—*Marigold*, Bethany mentally corrected—tried to push past her again, but Bethany stood firm.

"Couldn't you just say it wasn't you who made the charges?"

Jen smirked. "You don't think I've tried? They have security camera footage from the bank where she's been taking out cash advances. She looks like me, honey! The only way I can get rid of this debt is to declare bankruptcy or pay it off. I thought the latter was a better option."

"So you didn't care that she was blackmailing Ben to get the money?"

Jen stared at her like she was crazy. "Why should I care? First off, it's not even his money. Plus, it's up to her to pay me back however she can. She stole from me. If she has consequences, then they're deserved."

"Why did you decide to kill her, though? Now you'll never get the money." Bethany looked over her shoulder again, willing Charley to come through the door. Jen's eyes were wild, and Bethany began to be afraid of what she might do to get out of the office.

"I didn't *decide*. It just happened. She gave me Trevor's keys to return and told me she was going to the bank and then meeting Aaron's train on the way back. I believed her"—Jen laughed bitterly—"because apparently I'm gullible. But while I was waiting at her soup stand, I looked over at your kiosk and remembered that she'd dyed her hair the same color as yours that night after the poker game. She knew as soon as I showed up that she was going to make a run for it. She was never going to give me that check."

Bethany gaped. "*I* made you decide to kill her?"

"I told you, I didn't decide. You just made me realize that she was stealing your identity just like she'd stolen mine. Of course, she planned to spend a little longer doing it, practicing your recipes and perfecting the look, before she took off. I guess she needed to find a new victim once my credit cards were maxed out, and she chose you. You're lucky, you know. I saved you from becoming me." Jen absentmindedly ran her hands over the pen set on Ben's desk.

Charley, get in here! Bethany screamed inside her head. What could be keeping her? Had Charley misread her signal and stayed at the memorial? Or was she waiting for another reason? Realization dawning, Bethany groaned internally. *Charley was waiting for a confession.* Bethany needed to get Jen—she'd given up on remembering her name was really Marigold—to say what she'd done.

"So when Trevor asked you about his keys, you told him you didn't have them?"

Jen nodded. "I almost handed them to him, but then when he said he needed them to access the maintenance tunnels, I realized I could use the tunnels to get down to the platform and get the check from her before the train came."

"So that's when you decided to kill her."

"No." Jen's mouth was in a tight line. "I still thought I could convince her to give me the money."

"Then why not take the stairs down to the platform? You chose the tunnels because you wanted plausible deniability. You wanted an escape route."

Jen waved her hand, dismissing Bethany's theory. "It's not a crime to have a plan B."

"Um, it kinda is if plan B is murder!"

"It was an accident," Jen said stubbornly. "I grabbed her purse—*my* purse, by the way. You have no idea how annoying it was to see her flashing it around with my initials on it. She tried to hang onto it, but I pulled harder, and she fell backward off the platform. It was just bad luck that the train came at that moment. I didn't even stay to watch."

"You went back through the tunnel," Bethany said. "And out of the men's restroom. You and Ben must have just missed each other. Then you realized having two purses looked suspicious, so you dumped the black purse with Trevor's keys in it into the trash can. And you were back at the soup kiosk before anyone noticed you'd been gone. It wasn't until then that you realized the check wasn't in the purse."

Jen nodded. "I was shaking so badly, I could hardly serve customers, but then Aaron got off the train and found me, and that calmed me down."

"Does he know you're a murderer?" The words slipped out before Bethany realized how incendiary they were.

Jen's rage boiled over. She grabbed the glass paperweight from Ben's desk and charged at Bethany. "I *told* you, I didn't kill her on purpose!"

Bethany ducked as Jen swung the paperweight at her head. "If you didn't mean to do it"—she ducked again as the heavy object whizzed by her forehead—"let's just go tell the police it was an accident. Mar—Jen provoked you, stole from you..." She crouched, panting, waiting for the woman's next move.

Jen gripped the paperweight so hard her knuckles were white. "I just want my life back, and I can't get it back without this check. I'm going to walk out this door, get on a train, go back to Santa Cruz, get married to Aaron, and live a regular life!"

"I can't let you take that money. It belongs to the station." Bethany's eyes were trained on the makeshift weapon.

"And I can't let you leave this room, knowing what you know, until I can get away. I'm sorry I have to do this. I'll try to just knock you out, not kill you, but no promises." Jen stepped toward Bethany and swung again, but she was too slow; Bethany jumped out of the way.

"Look at the check! It's not even real—it's a decoy. The real check is already in the bank, in the historic restoration fund."

Jen set the paperweight on the desk and reached into her purse. Taking advantage of the momentary distraction, Bethany dove for the object and sent it flying onto the floor. "Charley!" she yelled, as Jen grabbed her by the bun on top of her head.

The door flew open, and Charley barreled into the room, gun drawn. "Drop her! Now!"

Jen released her grip on Bethany's hair, and Bethany stood, rubbing her scalp.

"Drop the purse, too," Charley growled, "and turn around and put your hands on the desk." Jen reluctantly obeyed.

"Did you hear her confess?" Bethany asked breathlessly. She scooted the pen set on Ben's desk out of Jen's reach, and Jen glared at her.

"Yup," Charley said, as she clasped handcuffs around Jen's wrists. "Jen Smith, you are—*ugh*, let me try that again. Marigold Wonder, you are under arrest." She looked over at Bethany and shook her head. "I am never going to get that straight."

Charley finished reading Jen her rights, picked up the purse, radioed the police station for a squad car, and escorted Jen out. Bethany followed behind. As she passed the door to the women's restroom, she ripped down the out-of-order sign. Charley tried to hustle Jen outside as fast as she could, but Kimmy spotted them right away, and her mouth fell open in surprise. She elbowed Garrett and pointed, and he almost dropped his tongs on the floor.

Bethany hurried over to the food service table. "Can you believe it?"

Kimmy shook her head. "I know I shouldn't say this, but I'm *so glad* it wasn't one of our friends."

"She was such a nice girl, though," Garrett said, frowning. "She and Olive really hit it off."

"You know what Olive says. Desperate people do stupid things. Oh, look!" Bethany pointed. Aaron had spotted Jen leaving Newbridge Station in handcuffs and was sprinting after her. "I don't think he knows. He really did arrive on the 10:55 that killed Marigold—argh, I mean Jen Smith."

Kimmy blinked. "What? I think you better break that down for me."

Bethany nodded, scanning the room. "Where's Olive?" Spotting her, she waved her arm, beckoning her over to join them. She motioned to Ben, too. "I only want to explain this once."

"What about Milo?" Kimmy asked. "He'll want to know."

Bethany grinned at her. "I guess if he wants to know, he'll have to come talk to me on his own."

"It's almost time for the service to start," Olive said, joining them. She patted Ben's arm as he walked up. "Ben's going to speak first, and then Jen will say a few words, and—"

Bethany stopped her. "Jen's been arrested. Or rather, Marigold has been. That's why I called you both over. This whole thing is because Jen stole Marigold's identity."

Ben shook his head, confused. "Before or after she was killed?"

"Charley arrested Jen for identity theft? Then who killed Marigold?" Kimmy asked.

"Let me start over—I didn't explain myself well. The person we knew as Marigold was really named Jennifer Smith. She stole the identity of a woman named Marigold Wonder, whom *we* know as Jen. The fake Marigold racked up over fifty thousand dollars worth of debt in the real Marigold's name. And then the real Marigold tracked her down to try and recoup the money, which is why the fake Marigold blackmailed Ben for the restoration fund check."

"Whoa!" Kimmy said. "I did *not* see that coming. So Jen—I mean, the real Marigold—pushed the fake Marigold in front of a train? Why?"

"Once our Marigold knew the real Marigold was onto her, she decided to run off with the money rather than giving it away. She was probably planning to leave soon, anyway..."

"Of course! That's why she dyed her hair the same color as yours"—Olive gestured to Bethany's head as she spoke—"and started making soup. She was turning herself into Bethany Bradstreet. Oh, poor Jen—I mean, poor real Marigold. She is such a nice woman, Bethany. I wish you could have gotten to know her."

Bethany snorted, remembering how Jen had swung the glass paperweight at her head. "Well, not *that* nice, because when she figured out that the fake Marigold was planning to leave on the 10:55, she went down to the platform to confront her. She might not have planned to kill her, but she was willing to do it—and she did. And she was also willing to let Ben go to jail for it, even though she knew he didn't do it."

"Can't believe we fed her waffles this morning," Garrett muttered. "A murderer in our house."

Kimmy looked at him sympathetically. "Don't feel bad. This whole situation has taught me that one bad act doesn't mean a person is all bad. It can mean they were stupid or careless or desperate in that moment. The real Marigold has to pay the price for her actions, but we don't have to hate her for killing our Marigold. We can just be sad for both of them."

"Very true, Kimmy." Olive squeezed Kimmy's shoulders with one arm.

"I can hate her a little," Ben said darkly. "I did not enjoy my time in the clink."

Olive's forehead creased. "Ben, honey, what are you going to say now? If you don't want to give a speech, I understand. We can just ask for a moment of silence."

Ben shook his head. "No, everything I was going to say is still true, even if Marigold's not the person I thought she was. Let's get this memorial started."

Bethany stayed with Kimmy at the food service table as Olive, Garrett, and Ben walked to the front of the audience, and the noisy crowd settled down into a low murmur.

"The soup was a huge hit," Kimmy whispered. "We're down to the bottom of the pot, and I think people would have eaten those breadcrumbs with a spoon if we'd had more of them. Marigold would have definitely copied this one."

Bethany looked over at her friend and grinned. "Good. That was the goal—make something worth stealing." She stopped talking when Ben moved to the microphone and tapped it, clearing his throat.

"Friends," he said, spreading his hands to welcome the hundred or so people who filled the benches. "We gather here to remember the woman we knew as Marigold Wonder."

Nice sidestep on the whole identity theft thing, Bethany thought.

"I can't give you her life history because I don't know it. But I knew her as a friend, and I can tell you—she was exciting. She lit up any room she entered, even a room as big as this one." Ben motioned, taking in the vaulted ceiling of the concourse. "If you met her, you never forgot her. Not her name, not her face, not the energy she brought with her everywhere. She had hardship, as we all do, but Marigold took what was good in life and left the rest. We can all follow in her example. We can all shine a little brighter. So I ask you, instead of mourning her, to enjoy your life. Breathe deeper. Love more. Learn from the people around you. Drive the long way because it's more beautiful. Plant flowers instead of grass."

Bethany smiled. Put some glitter on it.

Ben continued. "That's what Marigold would do, and for all the things she got wrong, that was something she got right." He stepped back from the mic.

Bethany felt her throat tighten, and when she glanced at Kimmy, she saw tears in her friend's eyes, too. Olive stepped to the mic and requested a moment of silence, and they both bowed their heads along with the rest of the crowd. When Bethany raised hers again, she saw Milo heading for her table, an eager look on his face.

"I was looking for you all over!" He put his backpack on the table and started rummaging through it. Caboose emerged from under the tablecloth and wound around Milo's legs, purring. "Forgive me for being late and missing out on the soup again, but—"

"Hold that thought," Bethany said. She jogged over to the Souperb Soups kiosk and grabbed the pot of spring pea soup that she'd left on the warmer. She brought it back over to the table and poured it into a bowl. "We're all out of the garnish, but I'm not letting you get out of tasting my soup this time!"

Milo took the soup and looked at her in awe. "You are amazing. I can't believe you thought to put some aside for me." He inhaled the steam rising from the top of the bowl and then set it down beside his backpack on the table and returned to his rummaging.

Bethany threw up her hands in exasperation. "Really, you're going to let it get cold now?"

"One sec." He pulled a bag of cat treats and a photocopied page out of the backpack. He bent to offer Caboose a treat, then handed the paper to her and picked up his soup again. "You read while I eat."

"Glad the soup tasting rates now that Caboose is happy." Bethany chuckled at the cat's smug expression and took the sheet of paper. "What is this?"

Milo stopped with his spoon poised above the surface of the soup. "It's a page from the 1995 Santa Cruz Municipal School yearbook. I requested it through interlibrary loan while I was doing research for the profile. Look at Marigold's picture." He dipped his spoon into the soup and took a bite, and Bethany watched him intently. He closed his eyes and quickly took another bite, and another.

He likes it! Bethany relaxed and scanned the paper in her hands. Classic yearbook photos. Marigold wasn't Marigold, of course—it was obviously Jen. Her beauty mark was in the exact same spot on her upper lip.

She put the paper down on the table. "What do you think of the soup?"

Milo scraped the last few drops from the bottom of the bowl. "It's perfect. Literally perfect for the day and for the occasion. And absolutely worth the wait."

Bethany's heart swelled with pride. That was the reaction she'd been hoping for. "Now you understand why I don't make soup of the yesterday. Every day deserves its own recipe."

Milo nodded. "So, what do you make of the yearbook? I don't think Marigold was who she said she was. That picture looks a whole lot like her cousin."

Bethany bit her lip. "Sorry to be the one to tell you, but this is old news." She caught him up on the fake Marigold's deception and the real Marigold's arrest.

"Shoot," Milo said when he'd heard the whole story. "And here I thought I was breaking the case."

"It's still breaking *news*, even if the case is solved! It'll make a great twist for the profile you're writing, anyway. You might get the front page."

"If I have my way, your soup will make the front page." He smiled, his brown eyes sparkling. "Hey, how would you feel about taking a ride with me this afternoon? I've been meaning to ask you since I ran into you at the library and saw your bike. The path along the Newbridge waterfront is world-class."

"It's one of my favorite places, actually. But aren't you going to be busy writing up your articles this afternoon? I assume you're on a deadline."

"You got me there," he said ruefully. "Maybe I could take you out to eat tonight instead—I know a lot of great places. Perk of the profession."

Bethany suppressed a smile. "I'm afraid I have dinner plans already." She stole a glance across the room at Ryan. Milo followed her gaze, and when Ryan saw them both looking, he gave a brief wave in their direction.

"With that guy?" Milo looked at her disbelievingly. "He looks straight out of the pages of *GQ*!"

Bethany bristled. She had intended to tell him that it was just a volunteer gig at the shelter, but his skepticism that a handsome guy would ask her out got under her skin, so she just nodded. *Let Milo Armstrong chew on that!*

His face fell. "So, you and him—is it serious?" He cleared his throat and fumbled for the notebook in his pocket. "Just background info for the food feature, you know? Readers like some little personal details. You don't have to answer." He looked a little tortured.

It was none of his business who she was dating, but Bethany decided to let him off the hook. "We volunteer together at the homeless shelter. I make soup, obviously." She lifted her ladle a little and shrugged. "That's me, soup lady even on the weekend."

Milo's face broke into a relieved grin as he scribbled in his notebook. "That's great, people will love that. How about tomorrow for that bike ride?"

"I might be free," Bethany said, a smile spreading across her face.

"So that's a yes?"

Bethany winked at him. "My answer will have to wait—at least until after I read the food feature. I can't very well go out with someone who doesn't like my cooking."

. . . .

. . . .

KEEP READING AFTER the recipes for a sneak peek of *Chili con Carnage*, Book 3 in the Death du Jour Series!

Recipes

Avgolemono Soup

Avgolemono is a classic Greek soup that has a broth enriched and thickened with eggs. The trick is to make sure they don't scramble! It takes a little bit of babysitting, but the creamy, lemony result is worth the effort.

Ingredients

6 cups chicken broth

1 tsp minced fresh marjoram, dill, or parsley

½ cup uncooked orzo pasta

4 eggs

juice from 2-3 lemons (about 5 Tbs)

1 cup shredded carrot

1 large skinless, boneless chicken breast, cut into cubes.

salt and pepper

Directions

Using a blender, mix eggs and lemon juice until smooth. Set aside.

In a large saucepan, heat chicken broth and herbs to a boil. Remove one cup of hot broth. With blender on, slowly add the broth to the lemon-egg mixture until smooth and thoroughly combined.

To the remaining broth in the pan, add orzo and simmer until orzo is just tender (about 5 minutes).

Add the grated carrot and cubed chicken to the pan. Bring the soup to a simmer over medium heat and cook until the chicken is done (about five minutes). Season with salt and pepper to taste.

Reduce the heat to low.* Slowly add the egg mixture to the pan, stirring constantly so the egg doesn't scramble. Cook an additional 30 seconds and then remove from heat to serve. Do not allow the soup to boil.

* If you're cooking on an electric range that doesn't have a responsive burner, remove soup from heat or move to a new, low-heat burner before adding eggs to avoid scorching and scrambling them.

Split Pea with Ham Soup

Just like your grandma used to make. This is perfect to cook on a chilly weekend afternoon due to the long simmer time required.

Ingredients

2 Tb butter

2 carrots, peeled and chopped

2 celery stalks, chopped

2 onions, chopped

12 oz dry split peas, rinsed and picked through for pebbles

1 lb smoked ham hocks

1 russet potato, peeled and chopped

1 Tb chopped fresh thyme

1 tsp brown or Dijon mustard

12 oz beer (optional—substitute water or chicken broth)

6–8 cups water

2 Tb apple cider vinegar

salt and pepper

Directions

Melt butter in a large pot over medium heat. Add carrots, celery, and onions and sauté until vegetables begin to soften.

Stir in split peas, ham hocks, cubed potato, thyme, mustard, beer, and water. Bring soup to a boil, then reduce the heat and simmer, uncovered, until ham and split peas are tender, 2–3 hours. Stir occasionally to prevent burning. You may want to set a timer for this, because burned split peas are pretty terrible.

When split peas are tender, remove the pot from the heat and remove the ham hocks. When they have cooled a bit, remove the meat from the bones and skin and cut it into small pieces. Return the meat to the pot, discarding the bones and skin.

Add the apple cider vinegar to the pot. Season with salt and pepper to taste. Heat soup to desired temperature and serve.

Epic Chicken Noodle Soup

This is the soup that'll cure what ails you. The humble broth is the key ingredient—use homemade bone broth if you can. I like to make mine in a pressure cooker (or overnight in the crock pot). See the following recipe for bone broth if you want to make your own.

Ingredients

1 Tb butter

½ cup carrot, chopped

½ cup celery, chopped

½ cup onion, chopped

¼ cup fresh thyme leaves

2 Tb melted chicken fat (or substitute butter)

8 cups chicken bone broth (or substitute regular chicken broth)

4 oz uncooked egg noodles

1 large cooked chicken breast, cubed

1/8 tsp cayenne pepper (optional)

salt and pepper

juice of ½ a lemon (optional)

Directions

Melt the butter in a large soup pot over medium heat. Stir in carrot, celery, onion, a pinch of salt, and fresh thyme. Add the chicken fat or additional butter, then stir until the onions are soft, 6–7 minutes.

Add the chicken broth and bring to a boil. Stir in egg noodles and cook until tender, about 5 minutes.

Stir in cooked chicken breast meat and simmer until heated through, about 5 minutes. Season with cayenne pepper, salt, and black pepper to taste. For a brighter note, add a bit of lemon juice before serving.

Chicken Bone Broth

Making homemade bone broth sounds like an intimidating feat, but it's really quite simple once you give it a try. Bone broth can be substituted for chicken broth in any of the soup recipes in this book. Three methods are outlined below: on the stovetop, in an electric pressure cooker such as an Instant Pot, and in a slow cooker or crockpot.

Ingredients

Bones from a whole chicken (rotisserie chicken bones work great!)

2 carrots, chopped

2 celery stalks, chopped

4 garlic cloves, peeled

1 onion, chopped

2 Tb apple cider vinegar

fresh herbs (thyme, parsley, bay leaves etc.)

salt and pepper

water

Directions

On the stove

Place chicken bones into a large stock pot and cover with water. Add vegetables, herbs, and vinegar. Bring to a boil, then reduce heat to low. Cover and simmer for 5–10 hours. Keep an eye on it to prevent scorching and stir occasionally. The longer the cook time, the better.

Strain the broth into mason jars or other heatproof vessel, discarding the cooked bones and vegetables, and cool before storing in the refrigerator.

In the electric pressure cooker

Add all ingredients to the pressure cooker and add water until the pot is about two-thirds full (don't exceed the liquid line or the pressure cooker may not operate safely).

Lock the lid and seal the vent. Manually set the pressure cooker for two hours (120 minutes). When the time is up, allow the pressure cooker to release naturally.

Strain the broth into mason jars or other heatproof vessel, discarding the cooked bones and vegetables, and cool before storing in the refrigerator.

In the slow cooker

Add all ingredients to the slow cooker and fill with water. Secure lid and cook on low for 12–24 hours.

Strain the broth into mason jars or other heatproof vessel, discarding the cooked bones and vegetables, and cool before storing in the refrigerator.

Nostalgic Tomato Soup

The classic soup from your childhood, with the added luxury of cream. And don't forget—a bowl of tomato soup is incomplete without a grilled cheese sandwich by its side. Add a twist to this soup with the addition of chopped fresh herbs as a garnish. Basil, thyme, or chives are all delicious options.

Ingredients

1 Tb olive oil

1 Tb butter

1 medium onion, chopped

2 garlic cloves, minced

red pepper flakes (optional)

1 can whole peeled tomatoes (28 ounces)

1 ½ cups chicken broth

¼–½ cup heavy cream (depending on desired creaminess)

salt and pepper

Directions

Heat butter and oil in a saucepan over medium heat until butter melts. Add onion and a pinch of salt. Sauté until the onion is very soft (but not browned). Add garlic and red pepper flakes (if desired) and sauté for a few more minutes.

Add the tomatoes (including juice). Use a wooden spoon to crush the tomatoes as they cook and soften. After about 10 minutes, add the chicken broth to the pan and bring to a simmer. Cook another 15 minutes at a simmer until the tomatoes are very soft.

Turn off the stove and let the soup cool for 10–15 minutes. Purée the soup using a blender. You can use an immersion blender right in the pan, or a regular blender on the counter. Remember that warm liquids expand when blended, so blend the soup in a couple of batches to avoid splashing it all over your kitchen!

Return the soup to the pan over a low burner and add the cream. Season with salt and pepper to taste and serve.

Spring Pea Soup

Bright, delicious, and unexpected, this bright-green soup contains no dairy, eggs, or gluten and can easily be made vegetarian by substituting vegetable broth and omitting the garnish.

Ingredients

1 ½ Tb butter

8 oz garlic ramps (or substitute scallions)

3 ½ cups shelled fresh peas (or substitute frozen)

½ cup white wine

3 cups chicken or vegetable broth

¼ cup parsley leaves

¼ cup mint leaves

juice of ½ a lemon

salt and pepper to taste

bacon breadcrumbs for garnish (optional, see following recipe)

Directions

Clean the ramps and separate the white bulbs from the green tops. Roughly chop each part.

Melt butter in a large pot over medium heat. Sauté the bulbs until tender, about 5 minutes. Add the green tops and sauté for an additional minute.

Add broth and bring to a boil. Add peas and fresh herbs, and then lower the heat to a simmer. Simmer 6 minutes for fresh peas or 2 minutes for frozen peas (to prevent toughness).

Turn off the stove and let the soup cool for 10–15 minutes. Purée the soup using a blender. You can use an immersion blender right in the pan, or a regular blender on the counter. Remember that warm liquids expand when blended, so blend the soup in a couple of batches to avoid splashing it all over your kitchen!

Return the soup to the pan over a low burner and add the lemon juice. Season with salt and pepper to taste and serve topped with a sprinkle of bacon breadcrumbs or a dollop of crème fraiche.

Bacon Bread Crumbs

Ingredients

4 slices bacon, chopped

1 Tb olive oil

1 cup fresh bread crumbs (blitz two slices of bread in your food processor or use panko bread crumbs)

¼ tsp red pepper flakes

¼ cup finely grated parmesan cheese

salt and pepper

Directions

Cook bacon in olive oil in a skillet until crispy. Scoop out with a slotted spoon and drain on paper towels, leaving drippings in skillet.

Add bread crumbs and red pepper to skillet and toast until crispy, stirring constantly. In a bowl, combine toasted bread crumbs with crispy bacon pieces and parmesan cheese. Season to taste with salt and pepper.

Books by the Author
The Death du Jour Series:

Crime Chowder (Book 1)
  Risky Bisqueness (novella, Book 1.5)
Rest in Split Peas (Book 2)
Chili con Carnage (Book 3)
Lentil Death Do Us Part (Book 4)

Other Books by Hillary Avis:

Kernel of Doubt (A Neela Durante Mystery)
The Season for Slaying (short story)

Stay in touch!

Www.hillaryavis.com
hillaryavisauthor@gmail.com

For free books, giveaways, sneak peeks, and early announcements, subscribe to Hillary's Author Updates. http://eepurl.com/dobGAD

Made in the USA
Columbia, SC
29 November 2019